AMERICAN HERO

QUINN
EISLEY'S
WAR

**Patricia
Gardner
Evans**

Published by Silhouette Books New York
America's Publisher of Contemporary Romance

SILHOUETTE BOOKS
300 East 42nd St., New York, N.Y. 10017

QUINN EISLEY'S WAR

Copyright © 1993 by Patricia Gardner Evans

All rights reserved. Except for use in any review, the reproduction or utilization of this work in whole or in part in any form by any electronic, mechanical or other means, now known or hereafter invented, including xerography, photocopying and recording, or in any information storage or retrieval system, is forbidden without the permission of the publisher, Silhouette Books, 300 E. 42nd St., New York, N.Y. 10017

ISBN: 0-373-07493-X

First Silhouette Books printing May 1993

All the characters in this book have no existence outside the imagination of the author and have no relation whatsoever to anyone bearing the same name or names. They are not even distantly inspired by any individual known or unknown to the author, and all incidents are pure invention.

®: Trademark used under license and registered in the United States Patent and Trademark Office and in other countries.

Printed in the U.S.A.

Books by Patricia Gardner Evans

Silhouette Intimate Moments

Flashpoint #151
*Whatever It Takes #228
*Summer of the Wolf #243
*Quinn Eisley's War #493

*Eisley and Company

Silhouette Books

Silhouette Summer Sizzlers 1991
"Over the Rainbow"

PATRICIA GARDNER EVANS

has lived in New Mexico all her life, and has traveled extensively throughout the West exploring old ghost towns, Indian ruins and abandoned homesteads. She avoids housework by spending much of her free time outdoors fishing, and raising her own fruits and vegetables. She gets inspiration for her plots and characters from the land and people around her.

FINALLY!!!

Chapter 1

"Bless me, Father, for I have sinned."

The hushed voice could be Heaney's. So could the silhouette he saw through the screen of the confessional, but he'd never met a gunrunner yet with a sense of humor. They didn't make jokes, even bad ones.

"It has been a month since my last confession. Since then I've missed mass, I was jealous of my sisters, I had harsh words with my husband—"

He stifled a laugh as what he realized now was the voice of an elderly woman continued listing sins. Apparently she didn't have much faith in the effectiveness of the communal confessions made during Sunday mass, but the joke was on both of them. He had sat here before and listened to unrepentant murderers, thieves and traitors, but never an honest sinner seeking forgiveness for her small transgressions.

It was Saturday afternoon, the time confessionals got the most trade, and, from the long lines at the four booths at the back of the church, it must have been a particularly sinful week in Belfast. The woman must have seen that there was no waiting at this one, but she had to be a stranger to the church or she would have known there was no line because the confessional hadn't been used in years. Whether the curtains were open or closed was of no interest to anyone, and, tucked away as it was in an alcove off a side aisle, it was easy to slip into unnoticed. The woman, seeing the curtain closed on one side, must have assumed that a priest was waiting inside, and he had no choice but to play the role.

"—and I spoke ill of my neighbor. For these and all other sins that have escaped my memory, I am heartily sorry and humbly ask pardon."

Memories of a summer spent with a great-grandmother who'd been a staunch believer that weekly confession was good for the soul—especially that of a twelve-year-old boy—provided him with the right words. "For your penance, say six Hail Marys and Our Fathers, pray a rosary and make a good act of contrition." His thick brogue sounded as authentic as hers. There were some, he thought dryly as he added the ritual words of forgiveness, who would appreciate a black comedy that had him cast as a dispenser of absolution.

He slid the shutter over the screen, and heard the complaint of stiff joints come through the thin partition dividing the wooden box as the woman labored to her feet. The curtain rustled, and he was alone again.

Shifting sideways on the hard narrow seat, he tried to maximize the legroom in the stall, but the action was more to ensure freedom of movement than because of any conscious discomfort. Compared to some of the places he'd passed time in in the past twenty years, the dark cramped box was a suite in a five-star hotel.

With a patience honed by years of practice, he waited. The heavy curtain blocking out the light was less efficient with sound. He heard the creak of the old wooden pews as the faithful came to pray, the thump of the kneelers on the marble floor, the clink of coins in the donation box beside the racks of votive candles. The church had proved to be an ideal contact point. As neutral ground, it provided the anonymity and safety of a public meeting place in a city where a fist-size lump of putty, a couple of AA batteries, six inches of wire and a cheap pocket watch could make the usual meeting spots like pubs, hotel lobbies and railway stations the most dangerous of all. The abandoned confessional offered the rare advantage of privacy in public, as well, and, perhaps even more important, the ecclesiastical setting reinforced, however perversely, his identity as O'Rourke, who was rumored, among other things, to be a defrocked priest.

O'Rourke was just one of the many names and guises he had adopted over the years, although he'd kept this one longer than most. More people probably knew him now as O'Rourke than by his true name. Sometimes even himself. His dry laugh was silent. When one of the few who knew the name O'Rourke used it, he sometimes experienced the split-second phenomenon of not recognizing his own name.

His hand dropped to his boot. Two sets of footsteps were approaching from the back of the church. They came closer, and he heard men's voices, pitched low. He slid the razor-edged ceramic knife back into the casing in his boot. They were discussing who was going to teach Father McCann's catechism classes while he recuperated from surgery. He smiled thinly in the dark. He'd learned his catechism well—not the one taught by Father McCann, perhaps, but one taught by experience where carelessness was the deadliest sin of all.

The Fathers decided a newly ordained young priest deserved the job. Why, he wondered with idle humor, would a man give up sex in order to work Sundays and wear a collar that choked him? A calling, some said. Oddly, he understood that, if not the answer.

The curtain stirred in the priests' wake, drawing the scent of incense burning on the altar into the musty cubicle, and thirty years vanished. He was twelve years old again, in another confessional in his great-grandmother's village near Londonderry, smelling the same peculiar blend of incense and dry rot. He smiled unconsciously at the memory. Catherine Mary Doherty Finn. Proud, tough and with a tongue as effective as a shillelagh, his great-grandmother had always introduced herself with all four names, to make sure strangers knew right away that she was a Doherty, as well as a Finn. He'd spent the summer running around with a mob of cousins whose degree of relativity only she could work out, acquiring a brogue on top of his

South Carolina accent, and never noticing how poorly her tiny whitewashed, widow's cottage compared with his parents' large, comfortable brick home. Despite the difference in their ages—or maybe because of it—they'd shared a rare understanding. She'd died a few months after he'd gone home, peacefully in her sleep.

Muscles tensing subtly, he sat up a little straighter. His subconscious had been monitoring a set of footsteps hurrying down the side aisle. They paused outside the alcove, then someone entered the other side of the confessional, and he slid the shutter back as the bench in the other half creaked under the newcomer's weight. This man, he knew, hadn't come seeking forgiveness of his many sins.

"O'Rourke?"

The high, reedy voice had the furtiveness of a dark alley at midnight, probably because that was where the man usually conducted business. "You're late, Heaney."

The soft words were spoken in a casual, almost bored tone, and Heaney felt the cold dampness under his arms spreading. "Th—there was a delay at the checkpoint. They were searching everyone going through today."

The man known as O'Rourke didn't acknowledge the excuse, although he knew it was true. He'd been warned that the British soldiers manning the checkpoints into downtown Belfast would be more conscientious after yesterday's pub bombing. That was why he carried only the ceramic knife. The metal detectors at the checkpoints wouldn't have sniffed out the Glöck, but the gun would never have gone unnoticed during a body search. "I trust there won't be any trouble tonight?"

"There won't be," Heaney said quickly. Sweat began sliding down his ribs. He'd been expecting nothing but trouble ever since the letter had arrived. Unsigned, with no return address, it had offered him the opportunity to handle the sale of certain items soon to arrive in Belfast. He'd known right away it was a setup by the British army who exercised control over Northern Ireland. Who could be wanting him to handle a deal that size? Then Taggart had paid him a visit. Taggart was a high-level officer of the outlawed Provisional wing of the IRA. Word was about, Taggart said, that weapons that had disappeared from a United States Navy armory were coming on the market, and that he was the man to see. He'd sensed Taggart's puzzlement that he had been chosen to broker the sale, but he could have told him that no one was more surprised than himself. Knowing the IRA's suspicious nature, he knew, too, that the Provos must have satisfied themselves that it wasn't a British trap before coming to see him, and he'd begun to believe that the letter might actually be genuine. He'd even dared to let himself imagine the size of the commission he would earn on the deal.

He stared at the dark shadow on the other side of the grill. The Provos were bad enough, but this one... He'd heard of O'Rourke, of course, long before he'd received the message at the pub where anyone who was interested in finding him could do so. Not that many bothered to, and certainly never before by someone like O'Rourke. It was rumored that he was originally from 'Derry, and his accent bore out that particular rumor as truth, at least. There were the subtle differences that marked a man as a native of Northern Ireland, but, from what he'd been able to find out, O'Rourke did only occasional business here in Ulster. About the rest of the rumors he didn't know, although fixing such a meeting in a church gave credence to another. He glanced uneasily at the ceiling of the confessional, half surprised a lightning bolt hadn't already come crashing through it. The man had a strange sense of humor.

Some said O'Rourke had been unfrocked because of a woman, others because of his politics, but those who knew him, or claimed that they did, scoffed at that. No mere woman could ever matter that much to O'Rourke. He'd just decided that pious poverty had little appeal; his only politics was money.

No one seemed to know how he had gotten into the arms trade; perhaps he'd used a secret or two he'd learned in the confessional. One tale said that he worked alone; another had him allied with Khadhafi or a Middle Eastern government. The only rumor Heaney believed wholeheartedly was the one that anyone who crossed O'Rourke had the nasty habit of dying. "There'll be no trouble," he repeated, trying to infuse more confidence into his claim. "You've met with T—the other buyer?" He remembered just in time that names were never used.

"I have." In the closeness of the dark box, he smelled Heaney's fear, but he felt no pride in knowing that the gunrunner was terrified of him, only a grim satisfaction that the identity he'd cultivated was that convincing.

"And you've made your...arrangements, then?" Heaney twitched inside his clammy shirt. It was a measure of the seemingly fearless IRA's wariness of O'Rourke—which brought him no comfort—that they had allowed him into the deal after warning off several others.

"We'll divide the shipment evenly. The other buyer will take the odd guns, I'll be taking the other leftovers. Did you bring an exact tally with you?" Heaney would expect him to ask for it, although he'd known long before Heaney exactly what had been stolen.

He saw a flutter of white on the other side of the grill. After adjusting the curtain to let in light but not the view of anyone who might happen to pass by, he removed the grill that he'd modified some time back. The list and the printout he'd memorized agreed— neither Heaney nor Taggart were skimming anything.

With the light, Heaney finally got a good look at the man he was dealing with. O'Rourke was Black Irish, with the ancient Celts' legacy of light skin, black hair and eyebrows and, although he couldn't see the color, likely blue eyes. His head tilted as he read the list, catching the light more fully, and Heaney saw there was a surprising amount of gray in the black, surprising because the man didn't look to be much over forty. The hair at his temples and his sideburns was still coal black, which did nothing to hurt his looks. He wore a dark shirt, black jeans and a leather jacket with the sleeves pushed up, nothing flashy, but, seeing the former priest, Heaney could believe the rumor of trouble over a woman. Only it wouldn't have been just one, Heaney thought sourly, and the man wouldn't have had to go looking. "Trouble" would have been only too willing to come to him.

O'Rourke looked up from the paper. "Who is your supplier?"

He'd guessed wrong. O'Rourke's eyes weren't blue but gray, like the polished surface of a mirror, showing him only his own face reflected back. Hardly aware he was doing it, he made the sign of the cross surreptitiously. If eyes were truly mirrors of the soul, O'Rourke's was empty.

The silence finally reminded him that O'Rourke's question still needed an answer. Expecting it, he'd had an answer all planned, but the truth suddenly seemed like a better idea. "I don't know. I got a letter in the post. There was no signature, no return address. It just listed the...ah...goods for sale and the details of their arrival."

And the minimum bid you're to accept, O'Rourke added silently as Heaney's sudden attack of honesty ended before he could mention it. Heaney was telling the truth; the gunrunner really didn't know who had contacted him. The news of the armory theft and that Heaney would be fencing the stolen weapons had come through the usual gray network, the one that didn't rely on satellite uplinks or fiber optics. He'd tried to trace the rumor back to the source—with no more success than Taggart had had, he was sure. All he'd learned for certain was that Heaney hadn't started it, which left the thief as the only other likely possibility.

He folded the paper slowly. This wasn't Heaney's usual kind of deal. In the story that he'd given Taggart, trying, no doubt, to inflate his own importance, he'd made himself out to be the supplier's exclusive outlet and intimated that this was only the first of many such sales. Taggart hadn't believed that any more than he would have. A dozen Uzis was Heaney's usual inventory, not a carload of ordnance that would fill any terrorist's wish list. He'd expected the stolen arms to show up somewhere around the Mediterranean, offered for sale by one of the usual dealers. The fact that they were in Northern Ireland in the hands of a small-timer like Heaney meant the supplier was new to the business, someone without the necessary reputation to be trusted. As in any business, reputation was essential, and the thief must have realized that without one, none of the well-established dealers would come within a continent of him or his merchandise. He'd had no choice but to deal with a man like Heaney, a man hungry enough for a big score to take the risk that it might be a setup.

"Did you bring any samples?" he said as the paper changed hands again.

Heaney carefully withdrew a small plastic bag from his coat pocket and passed it gingerly through the opening in the partition. He heard Heaney's soft "Holy Mother" when he handled the bag with far less respect. The salesman had to know there was no danger, but his irrational caution was understandable. Plastique was even more powerful than TNT; a block the size of the latest bestseller would blow a 747 out of the air. He bounced the sack on his palm to gauge the weight of the Ping-Pong-ball-size lump inside. Enough, he judged, to turn the confessional into toothpicks.

There was far more demand for plastique than supply. With the malleability of Silly Putty, it could fill the gaps between the circuit board and batteries in a cassette player, wrap around a can of hair spray in a suitcase, be rolled as thin as a piece of 35mm film. A piece the size of one film frame was enough to serve as a detonator for several kilos of gelignite, which was much cheaper and easier to get. Yet, despite its lethalness, plastique was the safest and most reliable explosive, far better than the unstable mix of fertilizer and diesel oil that was an IRA staple. Taggart would have wanted the deal for the plastique alone.

Opening the bag, he pinched off a bit of the dense, whitish ball inside, then rubbed it between his thumb and forefinger, testing for the characteristic tackiness and graininess. Finally he held it to his nose—just to be absolutely certain it wasn't Silly Putty, he thought sardonically. Satisfied with the faint whiff of petroleum, he dropped it back in the sack. The color was virtual certain proof that the plastique had come from the Hawthorne Naval Ammunition Depot. American-made plastique was white and so tightly regulated that it was next to impossible this sample could have come from another source, especially considering that Heaney had fifty kilos—over a hundred pounds—of it to sell.

He pressed the top of the bag closed and handed it back through the opening. Heaney wouldn't have any other samples with him. Everything else he had for sale contained metal, which meant he couldn't have carried it through a checkpoint. "Three hundred thousand pounds," he said as Heaney took the bag.

Heaney put the bag carefully into his pocket. O'Rourke's bid was fair, and, as he'd expected, exactly the same as Taggart's. The supplier would realize a profit of just over a million American dollars—less his own commission, of course. "That's acceptable. There's . . . ah . . . the matter of a down payment to secure the deal. Ten percent is what the other buyer—"

By accident his eyes met those of the man on the other side of the partition. Heaney cleared his suddenly dry throat. "Of course, a—a down payment isn't necessary." As soon as he got out of here, he was heading straight for the nearest pub and a good, stiff whiskey. He cleared his throat again. "Tonight, then, eleven-thirty, at the old docks, number eighteen."

"I'll be there."

Heaney realized that he'd been dismissed. Slipping between the black curtains, he tried to remember whether the closest pub was around the corner or one street over.

The grill went back into place soundlessly. He'd known for several days that the weapons were stashed in one of the warehouses lining the old piers. He could have taken them any time, but the guns were secondary; Heaney's supplier was his primary goal. After checking to make sure no one was looking in the direction of the confessional, he pushed aside the curtain and stepped out. He glanced around casually, then, on rare impulse, turned toward the side altar instead of the back of the church and the exit.

A tiered rack of votive candles took up the top of the altar. A number of the candles were burning, lit by those seeking a special favor or in remembrance of a departed loved one. He dropped a handful of coins in the donation box beside the rack, lit a candle from one already burning and set it back in the glass cup. The flame flickered, then strengthened until it burned brightly, for Catherine Mary Doherty Finn.

Several women were kneeling in front of the altar, and, when he stepped back, another moved to take his place, a slight figure in the habit of a nun—black dress, black stockings and shoes, and the regulation plain white wimple. Her head was bowed as if she were already at prayer, the starched wings of white cloth hiding her face. Someone else crowded him on his blind side and, instincts automatically on the alert, he was already turning away when the point of a knife pressed against his ribs.

"Keep moving."

He ignored the mumbled command to glance at the nun, to see if she was closing in on him from the other side. That was the standard play—two knives encouraged more cooperation. The nun remained on her knees, head bent over her clasped hands.

"I said *move*."

He paid more attention to the sharp threat in his side than to the half-hysterical demand hissed in his ear. Glancing sideways, he confirmed his suspicion. It was a kid, twenty at most, with greased-back dirty blond hair and a baby face. He was tall, but too skinny to have any muscle, and too jumpy to be a professional, but he wasn't really surprised by the kid's amateur status. With the way Heaney had been noising his wares around, the guns had become a bright light attracting all kinds of bugs.

The cheap jacket over the punk's arm hid the knife from view. Chances were he was acting alone. He must have been following Heaney, and, guessing that the arms dealer hadn't gone to church for the good of his soul, figured that a deal had been made and that it would be easier to persuade the customer to cut him in for a share. Holding his impatience in check, O'Rourke went where the knife directed him. Once outside, there would be ample opportunity to take care of this nuisance without an audience.

The opportunity came sooner than he'd expected. There was a loud crash of metal and breaking glass behind them, and the kid's head jerked around in automatic reaction, his attention, like everyone else's, focused on the chaos in front of the side altar. The metal rack that had held the votive candles lay on the floor in pieces. Most of the red glass cups had smashed on impact, littering the gray marble like splotches of blood. Candles rolled in every direction, some of them still burning and trailing tails of melted wax. The women who had been kneeling before the altar were on their feet and looking accusingly at the nun, who stood with her head down as if in acute embarrassment.

He didn't waste time wondering how she'd caused the mess. Driving his right elbow into the soft belly of his would-be kidnapper, he put several yards between them while the kid was still doubling over. The knife clattered to the marble floor, loud in the shocked quiet following the collapse of the candle rack, and he heard one of the women cry out.

"Look out! He's got a knife!"

He kept walking up the side aisle toward the door, moving at a pace that would appear unhurried to any observers, but a glance over his shoulder proved that nobody was interested in him. Everyone's attention had shifted to the young man on the floor, writhing feebly as he tried to regain the ability to breath. A burly man stood over him, the knife now in his hand. He didn't see the little nun, but she was no doubt part of the crowd at the altar. He hadn't seen the woman who had cried out, but he had the odd feeling that it had been her.

As he reached the narthex, two British soldiers burst through the doors. They'd come surprisingly fast, but then, in downtown Belfast, they were never far away. They didn't so much as glance in his direction as they ran down the main aisle to investigate the commotion. Without breaking stride, he continued toward the front doors. The kid wouldn't be stupid enough to tell them his real reason for being in the church, and no one else could connect the two of them. The British would detain the boy a day or two while they checked him out, long enough to keep him out of the way.

The nun was making good her escape, too. Head still down, she hurried toward a door on the far side. As she reached it, she raised her head and looked directly at him. The eye contact lasted no more than a few heartbeats before she pushed the door open and disappeared. His feet faltered for a step as the shock of recognition stunned him. It wasn't her face he recognized; he could recall no more than a pale blur. It was her eyes.

Four months before, those same eyes had stared at him across a seedy waterfront bar in Cyprus—after another convenient "accident" had also given him a sooner-than-expected opportunity to get out of another tight situation. A shipment of Stinger missiles en route to the mujahideen in Afghanistan had disappeared in Pakistan. He'd located them on Cyprus and had been negotiating their purchase when the seller had suggested adjourning to someplace more private, a boat moored nearby. Knowing that the man across the table didn't have a moonlight cruise in mind, he had demurred; then two of the seller's thugs had suddenly appeared on either side of his chair. Knives had been the deciding argument then, too.

The four of them had been passing a tableful of stevedores when the largest one accused one of the thugs of bumping his arm and making him spill his ouzo. He'd seen what had really happened, but the ensuing brawl made it a moot point. Pausing at the door, he'd looked for the woman who had jostled the stevedore, to make sure she was safely out of range of the fists and broken bottles. He'd caught just a glimpse of her, little more than an impression of slightness and dark hair, as she'd darted between the tables ahead of them.

She was at the side entrance, seemingly searching for someone, too. For the space of a second, two at most, her eyes had met his. Framed by a dense fringe of dark lashes, they were a deep blue, the color so vivid, so intense, that he could hardly believe it was real; then she'd turned and slipped out the door into the night. He'd had only that brief glimpse, but he would remember those eyes as long as he lived.

And today he had seen them again.

Chapter 2

*D*amn. That was twice that he'd gotten a good look at her. Blue Harrell unlocked the door of a rusting white Escort that was the clone of a hundred others in Belfast and tossed her wimple onto the passenger seat. Running a hand through the short dark curls that the wimple had flattened, she laughed humorlessly. Twice that she'd seen him looking. There had probably been a half-dozen times that she hadn't. He was the expert at this game, not her.

Leaning into the open car to give anybody who might be watching the impression that she was searching for something on the rear seat, she looked through the back window in the direction from which she'd come. A block away, barbed wire caged in the shops and offices of downtown Belfast, giving it the look of an upscale concentration camp. Cars were forbidden in the city center, because they might be carrying bombs, and soldiers manned the gateways to search the bags and sometimes the bodies of entering pedestrians. She scanned the traffic on the sidewalk. He hadn't followed her. Perhaps he had only seen her that one other time in the bar on Cyprus and didn't remember. If he'd recognized her this time—or any other for that matter—she seriously doubted she would be here now.

Straightening up, she rested for a moment on the open door. The weak spring sun was losing to a ragged army of gray clouds, and the thin light turned the rain-worn brick buildings lining the street the color of old blood. The entire city seemed to have been built out of the same brick, from the endless rows of identical houses to the crumbling factories and dock warehouses. No trees or grass grew between them, nothing green to dilute the relentless red.

The drab scene reinforced her own feeling of dullness. Some of it was due to the scenery, maybe a little to actual weariness, but most of it was due to simple hunger. Resolutely Blue ignored the temptation of the public house down the street. Neon signs advertising food as well as what she guessed were the most popular brands of beer burned in a window covered by chicken wire to deflect bricks and gasoline bombs. Breakfast had been a stale candy bar and instant coffee made with water from the bathroom tap, and she'd missed lunch, but even thinking about a real dinner was a waste of time. She had to check in with her contact, then get ready for whatever was on tonight's agenda.

At the moment, the sight of a pair of golden arches would have thrilled her, but at least there was a small grocery a few doors down from the pub. She pushed down the lock on the door and closed it, automatically checking to make sure the other three doors were locked, too. When she'd been issued the car, she'd been warned to keep the doors locked. The local boys, it seemed, had invented a new game, one even seven-year-olds could play. They would steal a car, then play chicken with the British Army patrols. When the young joyriders got bored with that, they drove the car back and held a neighborhood bonfire. Yesterday she'd seen a wrecker hauling away the scorched skeleton of one of their toys. Tired of the game, the IRA, which was the only real authority in much of Belfast, had begun applying its favorite discipline to the older of the young car thieves. The offender was spread-eagled and a kneecap shot off, at point-blank range.

The grocery clerk rang up her "dinner"—a can of potted meat, a box of crackers, a half-pint bottle of milk and one very expensive orange. Something from each of the four basic food groups, she congratulated herself with a grimace at the meager pile on the counter, then added a rum brownie from the stack beside the cash register. At the moment, her stomach was more interested in quantity than in quality.

Back outside, she paused in the sheltered doorway long enough to get the Escort's key from her purse. While she'd been shopping, the clouds had overrun the sun and begun celebrating their victory with a thick drizzle. So much for the fabled soft Irish mist, she thought ruefully as she sprinted through the cold shower to her car. The rain had turned the windows of the cars parked along the curb opaque, giving them the same blank look as the British Army Land Rovers, whose windows were blackened to make it harder for snipers to find a target.

The storm had brought on a premature twilight, and the car's interior remained dark when she opened the door. The dome light had burned out, Blue noted in vague surprise. Slamming the door on the cold rain, she dumped the plain black purse that accessorized her habit and plastic grocery sack on the seat beside her, snapped her seat belt closed and stuck the key in the ignition.

After pulling away from the curb, she glanced automatically in the rearview mirror to check the traffic behind her again, and her fingers went numb on the steering wheel. The eyes staring back from the mirror were not her own.

They were gray, not blue, the same color as the knife suddenly at her throat. She stared back, paralyzed by the realization of one of a woman's worst nightmares: getting into a dark car alone and seeing a man rise up from the back seat. After what could have been a second or an hour, blood began pumping through her body again; air moved in and out of her lungs, and Blue felt the hard plastic ridges of the steering wheel digging into her fingers. Consciously she relaxed her fingers. She might never have seen them at such close range before, but she knew those eyes.

"Turn left."

Looking away to the upcoming intersection, Blue pressed down the stalk on the steering column and

downshifted. It was the first time she'd heard him
speak. The brogue, she knew, was assumed, like the
name O'Rourke, although she had schooled herself to
think of him only as O'Rourke to make sure she never
slipped up and used his real name, even with a contact. What his true accent might be, she didn't know,
but the deepness of his voice, the dark smoothness,
was exactly what she expected.

That he'd found his way into her locked car didn't
surprise her; she'd observed him long enough to know
that locked doors didn't stop him. That she'd been
thinking about him didn't surprise her either; he was
her assignment, so of course she had to think about
him, to try to anticipate his next move, but to realize
she'd been speculating about something as immate-
rial as his voice, even unconsciously, irritated her.

He was crouched, not directly behind her, but more
to the middle, situated perfectly to keep the knife in his
left hand at her throat while his right remained free to
grab the wheel should she try anything stupid. He
didn't have to worry; she wouldn't. She drove in silence, following his terse directions. The turns, she
knew, were to lose anyone who might be following
them. After completing another, she glanced back to
the rearview mirror and the eyes that were still there.
She'd known their general color for months, but until
now she'd never been close enough to see that they
were a rare true gray without any hint of another color
or even the usual darker shade rimming the edge of the
iris. They were pure, opaque gray...winter eyes...but
not the winter of warm fires, holiday cheer and soft
puffs of white snow. They were the winter of bare

lifeless trees, empty blizzard-ridden landscapes and blackened frost-killed flowers.

"Left on Falls Road."

The scenery now was reminiscent of downtown Beirut. The shattered buildings were the battlefield monuments of the Ulster war. When the ashes cooled, the neighborhood children had another new playground. As she drove past a parish hall with sandbagged windows and doors, Blue cleared her throat quietly. It was past time to introduce herself, although she wasn't looking forward to his reaction. She'd been warned that if the occasion ever arose, he wouldn't be gracious about it.

"I—"

The rest of her introduction went unsaid as she obeyed the command implicit in the increased pressure against her jugular. Okay, no small talk, she agreed silently. There would be plenty of time for introductions when they got wherever they were going, and his last-second directions coupled with the slick, unfamiliar streets were enough to deal with at the moment, anyway.

He watched the blue eyes in the mirror shift away to the street ahead. He hadn't allowed her to speak to impress upon her that he was the one in control. She would speak only if he gave her permission to, would do only what he told her to do, would survive only if it pleased him to allow her to. So far she'd obeyed, yet the angle of her chin made him wonder just how much control over her he really had. A demonstration might be needed to ensure her continued obedience.

He maintained pressure on the blade, not enough to break the skin, but enough to remind her that it was razor sharp. Not for the first time, he asked himself the questions for which he had no answers—yet. Who was she? And why, twice in four months and in places thousands of miles apart, had she appeared to provide a diversion at just the right moment? Coincidence wouldn't explain her presence, even if he believed in it. He'd attended too many funerals of men who did.

Increasing the pressure, he watched carefully for a reaction. The muscle in her jaw didn't tighten; her firm mouth didn't quiver; her smooth cheek didn't turn any paler; her breathing didn't alter. His own had, he discovered, and he stopped himself from taking another deep breath that wasn't necessary. He already knew her scent. It wasn't the sour reek of fear, but clean and subtly sweet.

He relaxed the pressure on the knife. Whoever she was, she wasn't afraid of him. Reaching over the seat in front of him, he groped for the purse and shopping bag she'd dropped on the passenger side. Without taking his eyes off her, he snicked open the clasp on the purse and searched the contents by touch. She had been afraid, for the split second between catching sight of him in the mirror and recognizing him. Recognizing him shouldn't have been that reassuring, he thought sardonically as his hand closed over a cellophane-wrapped package. Too big for a pack of cigarettes, but the springy give of it when he squeezed didn't feel like anything to immediately worry about. He would search it, and her, thoroughly, later. His fingers identified the single key attached to a small disk as a hotel room key. He would check the name on it later, but doubted he'd be surprised when he read it. His thumb counted a dozen or so bills in a thin wallet and a few coins. There was a smooth, stiff piece of plastic, probably a driver's license, and nothing else— no papers, no photographs, no credit cards. In the side pocket was an almost empty packet of tissues, and on the bottom, a hairbrush and another packet of flat, flexible paper-wrapped sticks. He sniffed the packet, smelled cinnamon and nothing else, and dropped the chewing gum back into the handbag.

Setting the purse aside, he picked up the shopping bag, the plastic sack crackling as he reached into it.

"Please don't squash my brownie."

He managed, just barely, to keep from laughing out loud, as much at her prissy tone as at the words themselves. She could have her throat cut any second, and she was worrying about a *cookie?* Realizing abruptly that he had relaxed, he jerked himself back to maximum alertness, and with something that felt closely akin to anger, his eyes narrowed on the woman.

Blue swallowed a groan. She must be more tired than she'd thought. Sneaking a peek at the mirror, she saw no sign that he'd heard her idiotic comment. As usual, his eyes showed nothing. It was as if he were protecting himself from the human frailty of emotion...or maybe he just didn't have any. Perhaps nothing showed because that was what was inside— nothing.

Once they reached the outskirts of Belfast, he directed her onto a narrow two-lane paved road. They met no one on the road, and only the metronomic swish of the wipers and the steady wet hiss of the tires on the pavement disturbed the silence in the small car. Blue could almost have believed she was alone, except for the eyes in the mirror whenever she looked up, always there, always watching her. He must be part cat, she decided absently; he never seemed to blink.

The lights of Belfast receded behind them with only darkening countryside ahead. Blue began to suspect their destination when he directed her to turn left at the crossroads of nowhere to nowhere, and she was certain of it when he ordered another turn onto a muddy lane that cut through stone-walled, jigsaw fields. The day before, at dawn, he'd met two IRA officers at a deserted farm cottage. It had been the kind of situation she liked least. There had been no crowd to lose herself in and, with the daylight and open ground around the isolated house, no way to approach unobserved. She'd been forced to simply wait, too far away to know what might be happening inside the stone house.

"Here."

Turning off the dirt road, Blue followed a rough track, the headlights illuminating gray stone, bleached thatch and boarded windows. A subtle tension tightened her stomach. Introductions couldn't be put off much longer.

Without warning, he reached over the seat and jerked the key out of the ignition, killing the engine. At the sudden loss of power, the car lurched violently, and she struggled with the wheel. Only when her left arm suddenly became useless because it was

entangled in her loose seat belt did she realize he'd released the buckle at the same time he'd stolen the key.
By the time she got her arm free and the car under
control and stopped, he was out of it, her door was
open and the knife was back in place.

"Turn off the lights."

Blue stabbed the switch with her finger. As annoyed as she was with herself for losing her cover, she
had to admit that she was simply outclassed. She
should have known that she wouldn't get away with
letting him get a good look at her twice. His was an
intelligence and cunning that overlooked nothing,
made no mistakes. Her best chance for escape would
have been when he'd gotten out of the car and been
vulnerable for the second or two that it took him to
maneuver the knife around the doorpost, but he'd
seen to it that she hadn't had even that much opportunity. He'd known that she would instinctively try to
control the car when he cut the engine and, with the
added insurance of immobilizing one of her arms, he'd
given himself more than enough time to leave the car
while keeping her occupied.

Reaching in with his free hand, he hauled her out of
the seat. Again the move caught her unawares and
kept her off balance long enough so that by the time
Blue got her feet firmly under her, he was behind her,
his left arm wrapped around her, the sharp point of
the knife now poised at the softest, most vulnerable
spot beneath her chin. His right hand held her other
arm, his grip further encouraging her cooperation.
The hold was perfect, although she would have ex-

pected nothing less. There was no way she could get away from him without cutting her own throat.

His much larger body forced hers into motion as he started toward the door of the cottage. There was nothing loverlike in the feel of his arms around her, nothing erotic in the way their bodies pressed and rubbed together; yet something—a heat—seemed to seep from his body into hers, lessening the sudden, shocking chill of the rain, loosening the tight knot in her stomach.

Out of the corner of her eye she caught a glimpse of her purse dangling from his arm. It looked silly, she thought abstractedly, although the man who flung open the cottage door didn't seem to see anything funny. The large black pistol in his hand didn't look funny, either.

The unexpected appearance of the man made her jump; the body behind hers didn't so much as quiver.

"I thought we had a meeting an hour ago, O'Rourke. Why—who the hell's this?"

With the rain and darkness, the man hadn't immediately noticed that O'Rourke wasn't alone. She'd never seen him before, but she'd seen his twins in Beirut, in Lima, in too many places: all young, lean, their faces usually covered with black hoods or ski masks, their religion terrorism, their credo destruction and death. O'Rourke didn't answer, just kept them moving toward the door. For a second the other man looked as if he were considering blocking their entry; then he stepped back out of the way.

The door shut behind them with a hollow echo. It was dark inside, but a pale, door-size rectangle in the far wall indicated that a light was burning somewhere in the back. Without pause, they moved toward it, and a few seconds later Blue saw that the source of light was a gas lantern hanging from a hook in the ceiling of what had once been the kitchen. The room had been stripped of anything salvageable, and the only furnishings now were a motorcycle and, looking somehow even more incongruous, a leaking over-stuffed chair upholstered in huge pink flowers. An oily rag hung over the handlebars of the motorcycle, sug-gesting that the man had passed the time tinkering. On the seat was a black pack and beside it, prosaically enough, a thermos and a packet of cheese crackers.

The man followed them, dropping his gun on the motorcycle seat as he went by, and when O'Rourke halted and swung both of them around, he repeated his question. "Who is she, O'Rourke?"

"You tell me, McTier."

McTier. Even though she was under a roof, Blue felt the nasty chill of the rain again. There would be no introductions and explanations now. McTier had been one of the two Provos O'Rourke had met here yester-day.

"She's not one of ours."

"I don't like watchdogs, McTier." The soft, even words lifted the hair on the back of her neck.

"I tell you, she's not ours, O'Rourke."

"Then who is she?"

It was a simple question rather than an accusation, and Blue watched the tension in McTier's body ebb. "I don't know." He dared a slight shrug. "Let's ask her."

"Later." His dismissive tone suggested he'd suddenly lost interest in her. The knife and the hand on her arm were still very interested, though.

McTier began a vigorous protest. "Later bloody hell! We should find out who she sodding is right now and what she knows—"

"It doesn't matter who she is or what she knows. She's not going to be in a position to cause trouble." Blue felt his shoulder muscles shift and knew he was looking down at her. "You aren't going to cause any trouble, are you, sweetheart?" he repeated in a silky murmur.

The cold knife blade caressed the side of her throat, and in spite of herself, she shivered, but from the coldness of the blade, not fear. Blue turned her head to look up at him. As long as McTier was present, there was no way she could reveal her identity or her purpose; she must say or do nothing that could jeopardize tonight's deal, yet, despite the precariousness of her situation, she felt a peculiar sense of security. In the past ten months, she'd learned that O'Rourke was totally ruthless, seemingly utterly without emotions, but never had she seen him do anything sadistic or wantonly cruel. She was safe with him.

The tremor that coursed through her gave him a perverse satisfaction, yet the expression in those extraordinary eyes when she looked up at him was cool, composed, almost . . . trusting. "Sit down."

She did as she was told, and he released her. One hand started to move up as if to rub the arm he'd been holding, then lowered. She sat quietly, eyes downcast, her hands clasped loosely in her lap, and the satisfaction he'd felt a moment before became a sour taste in his mouth.

McTier looked at her uncertainly. "Maybe she is a nun?"

O'Rourke gave the younger man a brief look, and a dull flush darkened McTier's face. Taggart had assigned him the role of go-between to ensure the smooth coordination of tonight's sale. He'd joined the youth wing of the IRA when he was fourteen, been interned without trial on a prison ship, which was an almost obligatory IRA rite of passage, but he suspected Taggart still didn't fully trust him. His eyes were overbright, and his body was never quite still. Even now he was twitching in anticipation of tonight's action. McTier was an adrenaline junkie and, like all addicts, more interested in his next fix than anything else, but he did have his uses. Depending on who was telling the story, he'd either dropped or washed out of medical school, but he'd lasted long enough to acquire the surgical skill to handle the routine gunshot wound, and his knowledge of drugs, especially the more persuasive ones, was extensive.

"What do we do with her?" McTier demanded.

Blue resisted the urge to close her eyes and sink into the fat warm comfort of the chair. She was exhausted and cold, and she never had had a chance to eat her "dinner," which was probably why, she decided wryly, she was as interested in the thermos and crackers sitting beside the pack on McTier's motorcycle as she was in O'Rourke's answer.

Instead of answering, he asked a question of his own. "What's in the thermos?"

Watching through her lashes, Blue saw a flicker of impatience cross McTier's face before he answered. "Tea."

"Maybe the lady would like a cup."

The lady would definitely like a cup. Blue looked up hopefully at the dark man standing over her. Maybe his unexpected hospitality would make him equally generous with McTier's crackers. For once he wasn't looking at her, and she sensed that a silent signal had been sent over her head, but by the time she looked back to McTier, he was already walking toward her. The streamer of steam rising from the cup in his grimy hand killed any speculation on what the wordless message between the two men might have been.

"Thank you," she murmured as she wrapped her cold, stiff hands around the warm cup. The tea was too sweet, but she imagined she could already feel its warmth circulating through her as she drained the cup. Her hands relaxed; in fact her whole body suddenly relaxed, and the soft comfort of the chair became too much to resist. She sank into it, only vaguely wondering why the lovely warmth flowing through her was taking on a peculiar chill....

Finally she understood. Through the dark, cold cloud engulfing her, she had one last glimpse of the man looming over her. His eyes were clear and steady, the eyes of a marksman with the target in his sights, sure of the kill. Now she knew the silent message he'd sent, and how stupidly naive she'd been. She'd put her life in the hands of this man, trusting that he would keep her from harm, forgetting that he was the most dangerous enemy of all....

Chapter 3

"She looks a sweet bit of tail. I've always wondered what it would be like to—" McTier's choice of verb was predictably obscene "—a nun."

What McTier's vocabulary lacked in originality he made up for in frequency, O'Rourke thought absently as he stared down at the woman slumped in the armchair, unconscious and defenseless. She was an inconvenience. It was imperative that he find out who she was and why she'd been following him for months, but he didn't have the time right now. Drugging her had been the best option, and fortunately McTier was never without his kit.

McTier picked up the cup from the floor where it had fallen from her hand, rinsed it out with fresh tea and wiped it fastidiously before screwing it back on the stainless-steel thermos. "I nicked this off a dead British moth—" he began with the pride of ownership.

O'Rourke paid little attention as McTier finished the stock epithet. Just before she'd lost consciousness, she'd realized what was happening to her, and she'd looked up at him, a mute, desperate plea in those haunting eyes. With an abrupt move, he started for the front door. "I'll be back in a couple of hours."

McTier jerked around in surprise. "I'm not a bleeding baby-sitter, O'Rourke. I gave her enough to put her out for hours. She'll be here when we get back."

"Aye," he nodded agreeably, "because you'll be here to see that she doesn't wake up and wander off. Just in case—" he paused so McTier couldn't mistake his meaning "—she walks in her sleep." Almost idly, he waited to see if McTier was stupid enough to challenge him. Leaving the woman with the younger man while he took care of the last-minute details solved two problems. It saved him the trouble of losing the Provo, and kept her out of the way until he did have time for her.

McTier took a step toward him, then stopped, swearing with a vicious impotence. "I told you, she's not one of ours."

Silently he agreed. She wasn't IRA; she wasn't even Irish. The few words she'd said had had a North American accent. "I'll be back in a few hours," he repeated.

Turning away, he caught McTier's covert glance at the armchair. "Oh, and McTier..." He waited until he was sure he had the younger man's complete attention. "The woman is mine."

McTier crumpled the empty cracker wrapper and tossed it toward a corner. Staring at the motionless figure in the armchair, he swallowed the last of his tea. He would have liked something more potent, but Taggart had kneecapped a man once just because he'd smelled beer on his breath before a job. He packed away the thermos, then started across the room. He wasn't afraid of a man too squeamish even to swear. Not even a "bloody" or a "damn" ever soiled O'Rourke's dainty lips, he thought with a sneer.

Squatting down in front of the armchair, he reached out, but at the last second his hand detoured to the handbag beside the chair. O'Rourke probably hadn't even looked inside it, he told himself as an excuse. After giving a hotel key, hairbrush, tissues and chewing gum a cursory examination, he pulled out a small blue-and-white cardboard box. Opening one end flap revealed white paper-wrapped cylinders, and he dropped the box on the pile with a grimace of distaste. All that was left was the wallet, and he laughed softly as he saw the bills. Just as he'd thought; O'Rourke hadn't searched her purse. He tucked the bills in his back pocket, then pulled out an international driver's license for a Sister Agnes DuBois, from America. He searched the other compartments, then the purse itself, checking the tightness of the bottom flap. Finding nothing, he shoved everything back into the bag and dropped it beside the chair.

He listened to the night silence surrounding the cottage for a long minute before moving again. Her hair was soft. So was her cheek. His gaze moved downward slowly. There were even softer places.

"Everything ready for tonight?"

O'Rourke answered with a grunt as McTier followed him through the cottage. Dropping the blanket he'd brought with him onto the chair arm, he leaned over the motionless woman.

"She never moved a muscle," McTier volunteered.

She looked exactly as he'd left her. He had no scruples against drugging; he'd done the same himself more than once, and, awake, she would very probably have outsmarted McTier and gotten away before he could interrogate her. Yet he'd felt an inexplicable reluctance at leaving her helpless against McTier, a reluctance that had felt suspiciously like guilt, an emotion he hadn't experienced in years. Sliding his hands under her arms to bring her to her feet, he noticed a small smudge of oily grime on the edge of her spotless white collar.

The sudden pain that exploded through his face blinded McTier. After a few seconds his vision returned, and he stared in terrified astonishment at the man standing in front of him. He'd never even seen O'Rourke move. The wet warmth gushing down the lower part of his face was blood, he realized dimly. His nose was broken. He tried to step back out of range, and that was when he discovered that his knees had given out and that it was O'Rourke's hand, twisted in his shirt, that was holding him up.

"You were supposed to keep your hands to yourself, McTier." O'Rourke spoke as if he were chiding him for sneaking a sweet before supper.

"I—I did!" He shook his head in frantic agreement. "I never tou—"

He didn't see the blow coming this time, either. What felt like a lead-filled pipe struck the bridge of his nose in exactly the same place as before, and the excruciating pain blinded him again. What was even more terrifying than the unexpectedness and brutality of O'Rourke's attack was the casualness of it. He believed the rumors about the outlaw priest now; they weren't exaggerations. If anything, they were underestimations. With a masochistic curiosity, he looked at O'Rourke's hand as soon as his vision cleared to see what weapon he was using and, with another sickening shock, saw that it was empty. He swallowed back the nausea clogging his throat convulsively, desperate to speak before that lead-pipe hand could strike again. "Okay! Okay! I touched her! J-just a little."

"Where?"

"Her hair a-a-a-and her cheek and her—her—her chest." O'Rourke's eyes were the color of the freezing rain outside, only colder. "Through her dress!" he added in a panic. "I didn't take—"

The fist knotted in his shirt shifted higher, forcing his head back so that the blood ran down the back of his throat instead of his chin, choking him. "I swear it! I didn't—" His frenzied denial gurgled into an airless gasp.

Opening his fist, O'Rourke let McTier collapse to the floor. Picking up the blanket, he wrapped it around the woman. He handled her impersonally, able to ignore the fragility of the body in his arms, the fit of her head to his shoulder, the faint scent of her. Almost.

He glanced down at the pile of dirty rags on the floor. McTier's absence would raise Taggert's suspicions and risk tonight's transaction, so, as much as he would have liked to beat him to a pulp and leave him, he had to take him. "On your feet, McTier."

McTier scrabbled his way to his feet, his breath coming in a mewling wheeze as O'Rourke shifted the soft weight in his arms. He was taking the woman, too. She would be unconscious hours yet, and he could have returned for her later, but something, an instinct he preferred not to define right now—probably the one that had had him wasting time finding a blanket—compelled him to bring her.

Outside, he gestured to McTier to roll up the door at the back of the large truck that occupied the Escort's former parking spot. He climbed in, set his burden down at the back, then jumped out, grabbed the rubber strap to lower the door and locked it in place.

It was a few minutes past eleven-thirty when he turned onto the second dock and killed the headlights. The old docks and warehouses dated back to the last century, and most of the port's business had moved to newer facilities. A few of the warehouses were still in use, but most were vacant, waiting for the wrecking ball. Sparsely lit by the few night-watchman lights that hadn't been shot out, they sat in squat rows on narrow jetties, backs flush with one edge to allow ships to tie up and unload cargo, fronts bordered by potholed asphalt.

Roof sagging, its corrugated metal roll-up door streaked with rust, number eighteen looked no different than the others. Cutting the engine, he let the truck roll to a stop beside another truck as anonymous as his own. Listening to the suck and slap of water on the old pilings, he watched the shadows. None of them moved. There was the usual abandoned trash on the dock: a stack of wooden pallets, several decaying bales of rags or cotton, a broken bundle of 2 × 4s and a couple of fifty-five-gallon drums—nothing that would provide cover for more than one man. After a quick scan of the flat roof, he opened the door and swung down from the cab. As McTier opened his door, six men appeared from around the far side of the other truck.

"Lads."

"O'Rourke." Heaney and Taggart acknowledged his greeting, the others nodded. Wearing caps and jackets, they could have passed for ordinary workingmen out for a few pints down at the local, if not for the sawed-off shotguns. They were the preferred IRA weapon for close work, and every man except Heaney carried one. Besides Heaney and Taggart, the only man he'd met before was Massey, the ordnance expert. Both Taggart and Massey were third-generation IRA. The IRA had become a family trade, passed down from father to son or—very occasionally— daughter.

There were no introductions, but he hadn't expected any. Chances were the other three men didn't even know who they were working with. Usually jobs were carried out by a cell comprised of a quartermaster, who supplied the weapons and explosives, a "fixer," who handled intelligence and logistics, and a bomb-maker or gunman, or both. The men came together for one attack, then dispersed, rarely knowing the names of the others, so that if one were captured, he couldn't give up the rest. The fact that Taggart was willing to forget his paranoia for secrecy in order to get his hands on Heaney's merchandise was more proof of how important tonight's business was to the IRA.

"Okay, let's see what you've got, Heaney." The little salesman jumped at Taggart's command. O'Rourke almost felt sorry for the man. Heaney was so far out of his league, a rat trying to run with jackals. Scurrying to the standard-size door beside the roll-up, he fumbled a key into the lock while the others followed him through the shallow puddle of light cast by the watchman light overhead.

The sudden jerk of Taggart's head told O'Rourke that the IRA man had gotten a good look at McTier's face. Casually, he slipped his hand under the edge of his open jacket, ready to reach for the Bren 10 under his right armpit—his preference for close work, he thought dryly. Taggart's only response was to give him a brief, curious look, and he eased his hand away.

Inside the warehouse were several stacks of wooden crates, a row of metal ammunition boxes, Heaney's rusted Ford and a cot. Heaney was even sleeping with the stuff. Taggart ordered one of the nameless men to stand guard outside, while Massey put the other two to work opening crates. He gave a gas grenade cursory examination while Taggart studied a laser-light trigger that made absentee bombings even easier. With a lover's reluctance, McTier abandoned a submachine gun for the latest Glöck, a 9mm pistol made of plastic and porcelain, undetectable by the metal detectors standard in airports and public buildings.

Massey hefted a mortar with an almost boyish glee. "Now we'll be lucky more often, eh, lads?" The other Provos appreciated the joke. The IRA were stepping up their terrorism in London, and when the British had celebrated the failure of a homemade IRA mortar to do any significant damage to the Parliament Building, one of the captured Provos reminded them that the IRA only had to be lucky once in a while, but they had to be lucky all the time. He watched Massey exchange the mortar for a Stinger launcher. The odds would definitely improve in the IRA's favor.

Heaney watched as the men moved from crate to crate. Everything was as it should be, but still the queasiness that had plagued him ever since the letter had arrived increased. Relatching the lid on the last ammunition case, Taggart looked at O'Rourke. "What do you think?"

"Everything as advertised," O'Rourke said with a slight smile.

That one could give smiling lessons to the devil himself, Heaney thought, hunching his shoulders against the tomblike chill in the warehouse. In another hour this cursed business would be done. Perhaps he'd take a trip. There was a poster of Malta in the window of the travel agency below his flat. It looked warm and sunny, and they spoke English there. There was sure to be a pub where he could find a few lads to drink a pint or two with in the evening. And maybe he wouldn't worry about coming back anytime soon.

Taggart signaled one of his men. "Back the lorry up to the door." He turned to O'Rourke. "He can do yours, too."

He tossed the keys to Taggart's man. The offer was Taggart's subtle way of making sure he had no quarrel with the split. If one of Taggart's men moved the truck, he couldn't claim later that something had disappeared while he'd been gone moving it himself. O'Rourke watched the Provo back both trucks into position, then open up the backs. The man didn't show any interest in the blanket-wrapped bundle in his. He hadn't forgotten about the woman. She was there, at the edge of his awareness, as she'd been all along. Taggart knew about her, he was sure. McTier had had a low, intense conversation with his commander, but, beyond another curious look, Taggart had seemed unconcerned. She was his problem, not the IRA's, and, for now, his "problem" was unconscious and safely out of the way.

Blue arranged the blanket into a longish lump, then crawled toward the back of the truck, keeping to the sliver of shadow at the side. There was a guard pacing back and forth in front of the warehouse, but she noted him only in passing as her eyes instinctively sought another man. The tension stringing her body relaxed slightly when she found him. There were plenty of guns in evidence, but none of them were pointed at him.

She shook her head to clear away the residual fog from the drug and immediately wished she hadn't, as the throb she'd been trying to ignore worsened. The noise made by the back of the truck as it rolled up had awakened her, and she'd lain still, trying to orient herself while the man at the back glanced inside. He hadn't given any sign that he knew she was there, either because the light didn't reach that far, or because he already knew and didn't care.

The dull slapping sound of water and the dank smell of rotting sea life and old oil had told her where she was while she was still lying at the back of the truck. Automatically she flexed her hands, trying to work out a lingering tingle. She'd been surprised to wake up and find them free. No doubt because O'Rourke hadn't expected her to wake up so soon, Blue thought wryly. Still, the fact that he'd overlooked tying at least her hands had been a surprise, almost as much as the blanket.

Reaching up, she tucked the white collar inside the neck of the habit, then slipped off her shoes. They would begin loading any minute. A gun would be useful, but it was pointless even wondering where her purse was. The guard turned and started in the opposite direction, and she dropped silently from the truck to become one of the black shadows behind the stack of wooden pallets.

Counting the sentry, there were eight men. The stocky red-haired man was Taggart, the bearded one with the hawk nose, Massey, and the small twitchy one beside McTier had to be Heaney. McTier turned, and she wondered briefly what had happened to his face. The other men she didn't know, but she was certain none of them were O'Rourke's. He was alone.

Both he and Taggart handed over briefcases to Heaney. The Provos could easily kill him, take the money and the guns, yet, paradoxically, by coming alone, he was safer than if he'd brought as many men as Taggart. The sheer arrogance of it added credence to the rumors that he had powerful allies who might well take revenge, and then there was the other practical consideration: killing him would dry up a supply line that the IRA and others like them depended on. Yet, for all his seeming invulnerability, he was still a man . . . and all too vulnerable.

Now Heaney had something else to make him nervous, O'Rourke thought as he watched the salesman's hands dither over the open cases of money. Heaney wanted to count the money, but he was afraid of offending his customers by implying that he didn't trust them. Suspicion finally won out over fear, and he began to thumb through the neat bundles.

Raising the money on such short notice couldn't have been easy for the IRA. There had been three bank robberies in southern Ireland in the past week, the usual sign that the IRA was in need of quick cash. Profits from IRA-owned drinking clubs and "insurance" premiums extorted from the owners of small businesses had likely provided the rest, but they would recoup a good percentage of their outlay by reselling some of the arms.

Eight centuries of rebellion and guerrilla warfare had been bred into the Provos, but the old cry of "No surrender!" was taking on a different meaning as politics became less important than economics. The IRA kept the "Troubles" in the headlines, old wounds fresh and open, but railroad bombings now were less political statements than simple business tactics to weaken the competition and demonstrate the advantage of switching to IRA-controlled trucking companies.

Taggart looked at O'Rourke after they divided the last crate, and he nodded his satisfaction with the split. While Massey organized the loading, Heaney stowed the money he'd collected for his as yet unknown employer in the trunk of his car. When you were playing a game of double cross, it was always easier—not to mention healthier, he reminded himself with a silent humorless laugh—to know who you were playing against.

Blue curled tighter as two men approached, cursing under their breaths at the weight of the crate they were carrying. They passed by, and she shifted slightly, more out of reflex than conscious thought, to ease the cramp in her right calf. Although the rain had stopped, a chill sharp breeze cut through her dress, and her feet were past cold. She wasn't unaware of the discomfort; it just didn't matter. What mattered—the only thing that mattered—was standing ten yards away.

Most of the crates and ammunition boxes had been loaded when she sensed a difference in the night. The change was so subtle that it came only as a primal, intuitive uneasiness. None of the shadows moved, no noise couldn't be explained, and she was about to dismiss it as nerves when she finally realized that the change was in the sound of the water lapping against the dock. The even rhythm had broken into irregular, louder splashes, as if the wake of a passing ship were hitting the pilings . . . except that a ship hadn't passed.

Even as she thought it, she was rising from her hiding place, her mind racing, debating how best to warn him. Then, slowly, she sank back down into a crouch. Apparently he had noticed the change, too, his instincts more finely tuned than hers. A gun materialized in his left hand as he warned Taggart with a silent gesture. The first dark shapes were swarming over the far side of the dock when he threw the switch on the circuit box by the door, engulfing the warehouse in blackness.

Without his warning—or hers—the attack would have been successful. Coming up behind the cover of the trucks, the men wouldn't have been seen even by the sentry, and the battle would have been over before it started. Now, realizing that they'd lost the advantage of surprise, the dozen or so men rushed the warehouse, their automatic weapons tracing small bolts of jagged lightning through the night as they tried to regain their advantage with numbers and firepower. And their strategy might yet succeed, Blue saw with grim understanding. The IRA's sawed-off shotguns sounded impressive, but they were no match either in range or effectiveness for the assault rifles and machine pistols of the attackers. The sentry had gone down before he could even swing his shotgun around, and as she watched, another IRA man jerked up as if he were a puppet whose strings had suddenly been yanked; then just as suddenly the strings were cut, and he collapsed in an awkward heap.

She was glancing up to the warehouse roof when the heavy boom of the shotguns was abruptly replaced by lighter bursts of fire, telling her that the crate of submachine guns hadn't been loaded into the trucks. The hijackers dived for whatever cover was available, three of them not finding any in time. A ricochet chewed off a corner of the wooden pallet directly above her head, spattering her with splinters and graphically reminding her of the danger of her own position. She was unarmed in the middle of a firefight, and all she could do was keep her head down and hope that nobody else decided her hiding place looked like good cover.

The firing became less furious and more deliberate as both sides settled in for a siege. The nightwatchman light spotlighted the movements and hiding places of the attackers, and they lost another man before one of them shot it out. It exploded in a shower of sparks that made the darkness that followed even blacker.

The night seemed to thicken and close tighter around them, the blackness punctuated by orange flares of muzzle flash and streaking white sparks as bullets ricocheted. From her position Blue had a complete view of the battlefield, and when her eyes had adjusted to the darkness, she did a quick count. Even with their losses, there were still at least eight men left in the attacking force. A Provo had taken cover in each of the trucks, effectively taking them out of the fight. They could prevent anyone from seizing the trucks and the weapons inside, but their view was too restricted to allow them to be of much help otherwise. That left four men in the warehouse, although only three of them were returning fire. Not surprisingly, Heaney had disappeared at the first shot and was most likely cowering in the farthest corner.

Massey and Taggart had taken up positions just inside the door, while O'Rourke . . . Blue felt a chill that had nothing to do with the cold, wet breeze. In the seconds that she'd taken her eyes off him, O'Rourke had left the warehouse and was now about twenty feet away, behind the dubious protection of some rotting bales of rags.

White puffs of fluff spurted out of the bales as the hijackers found the new target, and she didn't hear her own cry. When the paralyzing numbness wore off, she realized that the rags made an effective, if unlikely, shield, much better than the thin steel of the oil drum one of the hijackers was using for cover. She heard the distinctive snarl of the Bren, and the shooter's rifle fell silent.

Massey ducked out of the warehouse and flattened behind a pile of lumber. With Massey's and O'Rourke's better positions and greater firepower, the odds rapidly improved. Apparently out of ammunition for the Bren, O'Rourke switched to the submachine gun he'd brought out with him, with no less lethal effect. The gun battle was quickly becoming a standoff. As well protected and supplied as they were, O'Rourke, Massey and Taggart could hold off the attackers indefinitely, unless one of them managed to get a clear shot.

Blue tracked one of the hijackers who seemed to be trying to do just that, moving from cover to cover, working his way toward the back of the trucks. Abruptly she lost sight of him. Certain that he hadn't been hit, she searched the darkness until, finally, she detected movement, more shadow than substance, under the truck closest to her. The man was inching his way forward on his belly and within seconds would be in position, and his first target was only too easy to guess.

The slight nausea of fear and too much adrenaline was something she hadn't felt in so long that she'd almost forgotten what it was. There was no way to warn O'Rourke in time. If she shouted, he might look first for her and give the shooter the second or two he needed. And there was the very real possibility that she might be shot herself. There wasn't even a rock, an old tin can, a board, anything that she could throw under the truck to distract the sniper and alert O'Rourke. Taking a deep breath, she readied herself for the one thing she could do.

Focused on the man under the truck, O'Rourke didn't see the dark figure coming at him until a split second before being struck. He had time only to half turn toward the blur, his gun raised to deflect any weapon, before impact. Spinning with the blow, he used the other's own momentum to help throw the attacker off, his subconscious noting during the scant second of contact a surprising slightness and softness, and a familiar scent. His consciousness noted the bullet that whined by his ear. As the small body slammed into an empty oil drum, he dropped and rolled, firing as he leveled out on his belly.

With the loss of another man, the hijackers recognized the futility of continuing the fight. Deserting their casualties, they retreated under heavy cover fire, and a few seconds later he heard an outboard engine open full-throttle. McTier jumped out of the truck in which he'd taken cover and ran to the edge of the dock to empty his gun after the fleeing boat. Venting his frustration at missing out on all the fun, O'Rourke thought caustically as he started toward the small dark shape beginning to stir a few feet away.

Pushing herself up, Blue let the oil drum behind her support her. Somehow it was no surprise to see O'Rourke crouched in front of her. His unreadable gaze traveled over her slowly, then met hers. "Stay here," he said quietly.

He was already rising and turning away as she nodded her assent. In truth, she couldn't do much else until she regained the rest of the breath that had been knocked out of her, but even if she could, she wouldn't have moved. So far, no one else seemed to have noticed that she was no longer in the truck and staying put avoided complications.

Even in the dim lighting he'd noticed that a bruise was already starting to show on her left cheek. With deliberate control he slid a full clip into the Bren. McTier must not have used enough of the drug, or she was resistant to it. Whatever the reason, she'd woken up too soon. Why hadn't she stayed in the damned truck, where she was safe? He jerked the empty clip into the carrier under his right arm. And whatever the hell had possessed her to pull such a dangerous, stupid stunt? She could have been killed. He slammed the Bren back into his shoulder holster. *He* could have killed her.

With an effort that annoyed him, he concentrated on immediate problems. If the gunfire had attracted attention, an army patrol would be showing up any minute to investigate. Taggart and his men were working double time to load the rest of the merchandise, and he grabbed one end of a crate to help carry it to a truck. As soon as the weapons were loaded, the Provos moved on to the casualties, theirs and the hijackers, to remove any evidence of the evening's activities. Glancing around, he frowned as he realized one man was missing.

"Where's Heaney?"

Taggart looked around, too. "Last I saw him he was trying to crawl under his car." He laughed shortly. "He's probably there still, waiting for his pants to dry."

Without responding, O'Rourke went back inside to find the little salesman. The lights were still off, but he could see well enough to know that Heaney wasn't still hiding under his car. The trunk was open again and empty, and, on the other side of the car, he saw the reason why.

Taggart came toward the car. "Find him?"

"Yeah." Heaney must have panicked, grabbed the money and tried to run. He should have stayed under the car, O'Rourke thought in angry frustration as he crouched down.

Taggart stared down at Heaney, already looking shrunken inside his cheap suit as the life drained out of him. "He won't be needing this," Taggart said as he stopped to lift one of the briefcases out of the dark pool spreading across the floor.

Taggart was right. Both of them had the practical experience to know, he thought mordantly. The only surprise was that Heaney was still alive. He was unconscious, and his skin had the greenish cast of death, but he was still breathing, although the liquid rattle said not for much longer.

"It's been a pleasure doing business with you, O'Rourke." The IRA man put two fingers to his cap in satiric salute, then turned and walked rapidly to the waiting truck.

O'Rourke checked the pulse under Heaney's jaw to monitor the ebbing flow of life, then grasped a limp, already cold hand tightly in his other hand. "Heaney," he called. "Heaney. Wake up. Wake up, Heaney." There was no way to save the man—he'd lost too much blood for that—but if he could hold off death just a minute or two longer, he might be able to find out how Heaney was supposed to deliver the money, information far more important than the money itself or the weapons, or the cruelty of not allowing the man to simply slip away.

He saw the woman before he'd sensed her. She stood a few feet away, touching distance, and how she'd gotten so close without his awareness disturbed him more than any of the other mysteries about her. Abruptly she knelt down on the other side of Heaney, as if she were going to make some attempt to save him.

He was opening his mouth to tell her that it was pointless when she raised her head and he saw that she already knew. Their eyes held a moment longer before he turned his attention back to the man lying between them. During that brief silent exchange, he'd had the odd impression that she was there for him, not Heaney.

"Heaney. Wake up, man. Wake up, Heaney."

The fine hairs on the nape of Blue's neck rose. The deep, compelling voice calling the dying man back, the silent darkness surrounding them, gave Blue the surreal sense that she was watching a medieval sorcerer practicing his black arts.

Heaney's eyes suddenly opened, unseeing and glazed at first, then gradually focusing on the man leaning over him. His lips worked for several seconds before any sound came out. "O'Rourke." His voice sounded as if it had traveled a long way.

"Aye, Heaney." O'Rourke's tone now was almost gentle. "I'm here."

"I'm dyin'." She heard resignation rather than panic in the faint words.

O'Rourke nodded, his hand tightening around Heaney's to keep him from drifting away. "How were you supposed to deliver the money, Heaney?"

"I . . . was supposed to use . . . the number." Heaney sounded distracted, as though the subject were unimportant. He gasped deeply for the air that his body was running short of. "O'Rourke!" There was a plea in his voice, as if he wanted something desperately but couldn't find the words, and Blue saw his hand grip O'Rourke's convulsively.

"What number, Heaney? How were you supposed to use it?" Urgency sharpened O'Rourke's voice.

But numbers and money were no longer of any interest to Heaney. His dulling eyes suddenly burned with a fanatical light, and his other hand clawed at O'Rourke, seizing his shirt in a literal death grip. "You've got to shrive me, O'Rourke! Please! You can do it! I can't die without absolution."

O'Rourke's eyes jerked up, and for a fleeting second she could have sworn she saw disconcertion in them. He stared at her, seemingly ignoring Heaney's frantic pleadings, and, not certain why she did, Blue nodded.

He looked at her for a heartbeat longer, then back down, and, in a gesture that might have been called tender, he placed his hand on Heaney's head. The dying man calmed immediately. "May God grant you forgiveness and peace," he said quietly.

They weren't the right words, but apparently they were enough. With a soft sigh, Heaney closed his eyes, and his hand went lax. For the second time that day, O'Rourke had found himself the unlikely giver of absolution. His silent laugh was without humor as he laid Heaney's hand on his chest. He hoped he hadn't damned Heaney even more.

Movement disturbed the dead air, and his attention snapped back to the woman, already on her feet and turning away. She'd gone only a step before he caught her arm and jerked her back around to face him. Finally he would have an answer to the question he'd had to wait hours to ask. "Who are you?"

The hand vised around her arm was large and hard-edged and pitiless, and the only warmth she'd felt in hours. Lack of food, exhaustion, a hangover from the drug and the rest of the evening's entertainments abruptly caught up with her. Blue heard the question with the same vague detachment she felt at seeing over his shoulder the shadows rappeling down from the roof and climbing up over the side of the dock.

When she didn't answer, he grabbed her other arm and gave her a quick shake. "I said, who—"

"I'm your guardian angel, Quinn Eisley." She smiled, a singularly sweet, oddly gentle smile. Then she collapsed in his arms.

Chapter 4

The lights came on with a blinding suddenness. By the time his eyes adjusted, Eisley was surrounded by six men in black wet suits. A seventh man, dressed in black fatigues, his face blackened to match the others, straightened up from the body on the floor with a smart salute.

"Captain."

"Sergeant." He acknowledged the British Special Air Services sergeant's salute with a brief nod.

"I thought we might have to join in there for a minute."

He heard the slight wistfulness in the man's voice at being left out of the action, but he didn't feel any sympathy for him, Quinn thought wryly, since the SAS sergeant's orders had been to intervene only if he were out of the action.

The sergeant looked at the reason why he hadn't returned the salute. "Is she all right, sir? My medic can see to—"

"I'll see to her." His arms had tightened possessively around the soft warmth he held against his chest; deliberately, he loosened his hold.

"Right, sir. We'll get on with the mopping up, then."

A minute later, Quinn switched on the interior light in the truck cab. The woman curled under the blanket on the seat never stirred; she'd passed from unconsciousness to a deep sleep without waking. He still had no more clue to her identity than that maddening exit line, but she'd used his real name, and the SAS team hadn't been surprised to see her. He knew now what, if not who, she was, and he liked having that particular suspicion confirmed even less than any of the others he'd had about her.

He dumped her purse out on the seat. The hotel key fit a door three down from his. Just as he'd thought. He gave the tissues, gum and false driver's license a cursory glance, then paused to thumb open the currency pocket in the wallet. The money was gone. He hadn't hit McTier hard enough, he thought dispassionately. The cellophane around the full box of tampons was broken, but the contents looked undisturbed, and one corner of his mouth curled. Too much for McTier's delicate sensibilities, and the checkpoint guards', too. He pulled out the short, paper-wrapped cyclinders and padding and hefted the small black gun in his palm. It was plastic, but no toy. Undetectable by security scanners, it was a classified prototype that he'd only seen drawings of until now.

Done with the contents, he started on the purse itself. Ignoring the bottom panel as too obvious, he ripped out the side pocket. The stiffening sandwiched between the two pieces of vinyl wasn't the usual cardboard, but a laminated identification badge. His "guardian angel" had a name—Blue Harrell—and she belonged to Damage Control.

"Nelson," he breathed softly, "you son of a bitch."

"Thank you." Blue took the mug and sandwich from the young corporal and set them on the arm of the chair desk she sat in. A few minutes earlier, he'd asked her if she would like some tea, and, remembering her last cup, she'd asked if there was any possibility of coffee. She hadn't thought to ask for anything to eat but—her eyes followed the corporal into the next room where through the window, she could see him dispensing the other mugs of coffee on his tray to the four men seated around a conference table—someone had asked for her.

The window between the two rooms had likely been installed as an attempt to lessen the claustrophobic atmosphere, because the barracks, like most British army posts in Northern Ireland, had no exterior windows. She'd awakened just as they'd arrived, and, with the "suggestion" that she sit down and stay there, Quinn Eisley had left her in what seemed to be a briefing room before joining the others next door.

She watched the corporal hand around packets of sugar and a half-pint carton of milk. Even before he did it, she knew the tallest man would add half a packet of sugar and no milk to his mug. Just as she knew that, were he in a bar, he would drink Guinness stout or the equally vile-tasting ouzo, not Irish whiskey or a martini—shaken or stirred. He raised the mug to his mouth. Just as she knew that he would drink half the coffee—or stout or ouzo—immediately, then sip slowly at the rest. Just as she knew he would sit as he sat now, motionless, no finger tapping, no foot swinging, no nervous or impatient twitches of any kind, just...waiting. It was the men with him who usually showed a few twitches after a couple of minutes. She knew his habits, Blue thought, just as a wife knew her husband's. The thought wasn't accompanied by the dry humor it should have been, but a peculiar, almost warning prickle instead.

Since there was no one to impress with her manners, she inhaled the sandwich, then wrapped her hands around the warm mug. Quinn Eisley. Saying his name out loud, just once, had been the magic invocation—or curse—that undid all the months of disciplining herself to call him, to think of him, as O'Rourke. And all that self-discipline hadn't been only for his protection. As O'Rourke, he wasn't quite real, just as the identity he'd adopted wasn't real, while Quinn Eisley... It made her annoyed with herself to have to admit that she'd used such a childish trick because the real man was all too real.

With a soundless sigh, she stared at the mud-brown Formica desktop. He hadn't called her by any name yet, although the condition of her purse indicated there was no need to introduce herself.

The men's voices came through the glass as a muted murmur. She knew the two from MI5, the shadowy service that guarded Britain's domestic security, and, while she didn't know the fourth man, the lack of any insignia or rank on his black fatigues indicated that he'd been part of the SAS backup at the warehouse. She could join them if she wished; indeed, Quinn Eisley had seemed to expect that she would want to, but she didn't. Her mouth curled slightly. He'd probably told her to stay here because he didn't want her out of his sight, not to mention reach. Her part was done, and exhaustion far outweighed her curiosity. She raised her eyes to the window across the room. And he could still see her.

He should have ordered another sandwich, Quinn thought, turning away from the window as someone else entered the conference room. It was the SAS officer in charge of picking up Taggart and his men, dressed in a regular British army uniform.

"How did it go, Lieutenant?"

The lieutenant answered the question from the senior MI5 man, Hollister, in a slight Scots accent. "Quick and nasty, sir. We got all the weapons back, but one of them's gone missing. He slipped away during the fight." The lieutenant sounded disgusted with himself and his men.

Quinn looked at him sharply. "Which one?"

"Dark-haired, skinny, smashed face. The others seemed to have forgotten his name," he said dryly.

"McTier." The name was a rank taste in his mouth.

"Don't worry about him," Hollister said with a grim cheerfulness. "The Provos are no doubt wondering why an army patrol just happened to run across them. McTier shows his face, smashed or not, he's a dead man."

Naismith, the other MI5 man, spoke. "Any casualties, Lieutenant?"

"One of the Provos won't stand in the dock, but he was the only fatality. One of my men got a nick. The surgeon's seeing to him now."

As if hearing his cue, a stocky, graying major walked through the door. "Anybody in here in need of a Band-Aid? If not, I'm off."

Not getting any takers, the doctor flapped a hand in farewell as a jaw-springing yawn overtook him. Quinn caught up with him in the hallway. "Would you check over the woman in the next room, Major?"

"So she's with you." Quinn realized the doctor wasn't as sleepy as he seemed. "She looks like she's had a hard night. What happened to her?"

"She was drugged and knocked around."

The doctor's brown eyes were wide awake now. "Who drugged her and knocked her around?"

He met the other man's hard stare. "I did."

Blue watched a twinkle traveling slowly across the black ink sky. After the British army doctor had prescribed the usual precautions, she'd decided she'd had enough of the claustrophobic barracks and found an outside back door. The wind that had blown away the rain had cleared the cobwebs from her head and even managed to give her the illusion of energy.

The door opened behind her.

"I thought I told you to sit and stay there."

She allowed several seconds to pass before she turned around. Wearing the same black jeans and leather jacket he'd worn for the past twenty-four hours, and with a day's worth of dark stubble, he was much better looking than he had any right to be. "I don't heel very well, either," she said mildly.

The glint of humor she thought she saw was no doubt a trick of the bulb over the door. He opened the door wider in an obvious command. Casually, Blue folded her arms over her chest. "You give a lot of orders," she observed.

He let the door slam shut. "And you don't follow them very well."

Now that he'd lost the brogue, she could hear a hint of grits and magnolias. "One of my worst habits." Her smile was unapologetic.

Putting his hands in his pockets, he studied her, apparently no longer in any hurry to go back inside. Perversely, she began to be. "You're not afraid of me, are you." It was a statement, not a question.

She shook her head with a smaller smile. "No, I'm not." Brushing past him, she reached for the door.

His palm flattened on the steel door, his arm across her chest, barring her way. "You should be."

She raised her eyes to his, so close that she could see herself trapped in the black centers, and a fine shiver ran through her. "I know," she said softly.

They went through the building, bypassing the briefing room and now-empty conference room, and he answered the question in her glance. "We're leaving. Our plane's ready."

In front of the barracks a Land Rover waited to take them to the airstrip. The two MI5 men, Hollister and Naismith, stood beside the vehicle, Hollister beating his junior by a half step to the rear door to open it. Eisley knew the gallant gesture wasn't meant for him.

"Goodbye, Mrs. Harrell. I sincerely hope we have the chance to work together again soon," Hollister said as he handed her in.

Mrs? Eisley's gaze sharpened on the woman murmuring her goodbyes. He'd known she was a temp—there were no field women in Damage Control—but he'd assumed that she had come from Naval Intelligence, the usual source on those rare occasions when a woman was necessary for a mission. Civilians were never used, yet, with the British exactitude for ranks and titles, he knew Hollister hadn't made a mistake. And somehow he knew, too, that the Mrs. wasn't left over from a divorce. Blue Harrell was somebody's wife.

Minutes later the Land Rover pulled up beside a small and sleek white jet with no markings except the black numbers and letters near the tail. Blue picked up the suitcase that someone had retrieved from her hotel room and climbed out, then crossed the few feet of damp tarmac to the plane. She'd flown in it before, although never, of course, with the man climbing the steps behind her. He paused to exchange a few words with the pilot while she stowed her bag and sat down, then, as the jet began to taxi, he took the seat across from hers. The plane lifted off smoothly, and she started to relax into the deep, plush seat.

"What does your husband think of your work, Mrs. Harrell?"

It was the first time he'd spoken to her since telling her that the plane was ready. Blue turned her head to look at him. "My husband died three years ago, Captain Eisley."

She said it as if she were giving a stranger the time, then she turned away, leaned back in her seat and closed her eyes. Closed him out. She seemed to fall asleep within seconds, and, from the slow rise and fall of her chest, Quinn knew she wasn't pretending. He was punchy from too little sleep and too much adrenaline, yet sleep eluded him. Where had Nelson found her? Wherever he'd gotten her, she was good. His ego wasn't so inflated that he thought he was infallible, but the truth was, nobody had ever been able to get close to him without his knowledge, and she had been following him for four months, had been close enough to touch him God knew how many times, and he'd never even suspected. Another "coincidence" in Marrakech suddenly came back to him, and he had the lowering suspicion that it had been much longer than four months.

Abruptly he realized he was still watching her breasts rise and fall under the black nun's habit, and he jerked his eyes forward. The derisive curl of his mouth was only partly for his voyeurism. As much as he hated admitting it even to himself, his professional pride was wounded. Nelson had wanted to foist protection on him a year ago, but he thought he'd put an end to that bad idea. He preferred to work alone, because he wouldn't allow his life to be dependent on anyone else for the simple reason that he didn't trust anyone else. Conceding that he hadn't known he was dependent on Blue Harrell did little to lessen the galling truth. Neither did the fact that it could be argued that her help had been unnecessary. There was always the chance that something could go wrong; she had been the wild card that had decided the odds wholly in his favor.

With a sigh that was almost a moan, she turned toward him in her sleep, and he was looking at her before he realized it. He didn't look away this time, indulging a need that he didn't fully understand and, uncharacteristically, didn't try to. Her mouth was a pale rose and even softer looking in sleep. Her cheek looked softer, the bruise standing out obscenely against the ivory perfection. Her lashes were straight and long, lush in contrast to the delicate tracings of her eyebrows. He still didn't know if her hair was black or very dark brown; he would have to see it in sunlight. It was cut in short, loose curls that lay close on her cheek and the nape of her neck. His fingers twitched. Her hair had brushed his throat when he'd held her— soft, silky, rain sweet.

She wasn't beautiful, whatever the hell beautiful was. She was ... pretty. It was a word that seemed to have fallen out of favor in describing a woman. Now they were *striking, attractive, arresting,* as if *pretty* somehow implied that the woman was second-rate, nothing out of the ordinary. There was nothing second-rate about Blue Harrell . . . and something very much out of the ordinary.

Her right hand lay on her thigh, the fingers relaxed. The cabin light overhead illuminated her palm, and he felt a sudden, crawling sickness in his gut. Instead of smooth pink skin, there were patches of shiny, puckered white scar tissue, some of them roughly circular, others long and narrow. The scars were from burns, deep burns. One of them followed the lifeline, extending beyond to her wrist. Cutting through some of the scar tissue and the healthy skin were thinner scars, red fading to white, that looked as if she'd been slashed with something very sharp and jagged. Her fingers hadn't been spared, either.

Even as his mind fought against it, he knew what he was looking at. He tried to think of another explanation—an accident, some kind of industrial injury, anything—but he was too familiar with the results of torture not to recognize them. Leaning across the aisle, he picked up her left hand with exquisite care and turned it palm up. It was the same as the right. He tried to view the scars analytically; from the degree of healing and color, they weren't recent, but several years old. He tried, but rage, much worse than when he'd realized McTier had put his filthy hands on her, destroyed his attempt at detachment. Very gently he laid her hand back in her lap.

From the first time he'd seen her in that dive in Cyprus, and even when he wasn't certain that she wasn't a threat to him, he'd had the inexplicable desire to protect her. He knew now who and what she was . . . and she was more of a mystery than ever.

And she was nobody's wife.

Chapter 5

"Next time, at least kiss me before you screw me."

John Nelson regarded the man on the other side of his desk with a bland stare. "I prefer redheads."

With a harsh laugh, Quinn took a chair.

He'd taken a chance on Quinn Eisley ten years ago, Nelson knew. Anonymity was a chief requisite in their business; a nondescript face and build made a man invisible, and, too big and too good-looking, Eisley would never be invisible. He'd been warned that he wasn't a team player, either. In the SEALs, where he'd gone after graduation from the Naval Academy and where team spirit was almost sacrosanct, he'd won a reputation as a loner, yet when his recon squad had been caught deep in hostile territory, he hadn't lost a man. When the helicopters rescued them the next day, the pilots had counted ninety-three enemy dead.

Eventually he'd advanced to SEAL Team Six, a cloaked counterterrorist force, and come to Nelson's attention as a possible recruit. The man's loyalty was unquestionable, his commitment total, his courage unchallenged, his intelligence and skills virtually unmatched. He had a sixth sense that was pure suspicion, developed in the Southeast Asian jungles where he'd first learned how to survive as prey as well as predator. He left as little to chance as humanly— sometimes seemingly inhumanly—possible. He exhibited the self-confidence—some said arrogance—to go into a room with half a dozen men laying for him, completely certain that he would handle them all. Because he had. He was the quintessential professional. "What do you think of her?" Nelson asked.

John Nelson, Quinn thought, was incontrovertible proof that appearances were deceiving. He looked like Santa Claus in a pin-striped suit. In reality, he was ruthless, profane and canny; *jolly* was the last word anyone would ever use for him. He had spent his life in intelligence, becoming the head of Damage Control when a nervous president wanted civilian oversight of military operations. Created as the Cold War was heating up, Damage Control was a very small, off-the-books operation of U.S. Naval Intelligence. Headquarters wasn't a country estate at Langley or Quantico, but a featureless gray building in downtown Washington. The name came from an old navy term for containing and repairing the damage from a torpedo attack, but this Damage Control worked to contain the damage and clean up the mess from torpedoes of a different kind, the ones known in officialese as "unfortunate incidents." "She's very good," Quinn said. "Who is she?"

"She's the daughter—adopted daughter, actually—of old friends. She was about two when her mother died in Tangiers. No family, father unknown." Nelson shrugged. "The usual story. Louis Beneux was in French Intelligence, stationed in Algeria the same time I was. He and his wife couldn't have children, and they adopted her. A few years later Louis was posted here to handle security at the French embassy." Quinn saw a rare smile. "She was six and decided immediately that she was going to be an American. She even Americanized her name, insisted on being called Blue instead of Bleuzette. Ridiculous, of course, with her eyes, but there was no arguing with her."

Quinn worked to keep his expression blank. Nelson was the master of oblique answers to straight questions, and he'd expected the usual terse sentence that would have done little to satisfy his curiosity, not an expansiveness that was totally out of character, even more so because the subject was personal. Nelson never discussed personal topics; there was never even a hint that he had a life beyond Damage Control. In his cluttered office, the only object that could have been considered remotely personal was a black-and-white photograph that had sat on the third shelf of one bookcase until a year or so ago. It was of an unknown woman, taken, judging from the hairstyle, clothing and graininess characteristic of telephoto lenses back then, in the fifties.

"After she graduated from college, she was with the D.C. Police Department for a while before moving over to the Justice Department. Then she married a lawyer specializing in international law and moved to Paris. They came back three years ago, when their son Ben was two, and bought an old farmhouse and ten acres in Virginia."

She had a son. A peculiar feeling, almost a pain, cut through him. He hadn't considered that she might have a child, fathered by another man.

"Her parents died in a car accident right after they came back, and three months later her husband and son died."

"What happened?" Quinn asked quietly, not wanting, now especially, to jar Nelson out of his talkative mood.

"A fire. There was a thunderstorm one night. Lightning struck the house. It was engulfed in seconds. Blue started after the baby, but her husband must have realized there was no chance. He threw her out their second-story bedroom window, and she broke both ankles when she landed. The firemen found her crawling up what was left of the porch, trying to get back inside."

Nelson's matter-of-fact recitation didn't go into details, but he could all too easily supply them: the howling roar of the ravenous flames, the lung-shriveling heat, the suffocating smoke. She would have fought her husband to reach their child. It was a primal instinct for a parent to save a child in danger, and he didn't have to be told that her husband, too, had tried to save his son, but only after he'd saved his wife, the only way he could, by taking the chance that he might well kill her in the attempt. Quinn couldn't imagine the depth of emotion that would drive a man to such a desperate act.

Yet, despite the grievous loss and injuries she'd suffered, he felt an oddly profound relief for her. The scars on her hands weren't the result of deliberate torture, but the attempt to save her family. She would have been in shock and never felt the slash of the heat-shattered glass or the hot cinders scorching deep into her hands.

"The bullet you took in Beirut last year proved you needed someone to watch your back, whether—" Nelson gave him an acerbic look "—you wanted it or not, and Blue was available. She was already trained in surveillance and infiltration. All she needed was a little retraining to tune up her skills."

Quinn nodded his tacit acceptance of the explanation. Selecting someone unknown to him was logical, yet all his instincts told him that logic and "availability" weren't the primary reasons Nelson had chosen her; the real reason was personal. As he'd talked, the habitual blue ice of Nelson's eyes had shown signs of a thaw, making him wonder if Nelson's feelings for Blue were only avuncular, but as soon as the thought came, he dismissed it. There was nothing sexual in Nelson's tone or look, no secret hunger, no suppressed desire.

Nelson glanced at the old Rolex on his wrist, then, with a briskness surprising for a man of his age and bulk, stood up. "Everyone should be here. Let's go see if we can figure out what the hell we're going to do now.''

His back was to her, the door was already open, and Blue knew she hadn't made a sound walking down the carpeted hall, yet cool, still gray eyes found her before she took the first step into the room. She felt the fine tension, a heightening of awareness that she didn't need—or want. The five other men seated around the oblong table looked toward her then. From their lack of surprise, it was obvious that John had already explained who she was.

Except for John, the men were in uniform, the starched khaki and razor-edged creases making her linen slacks and shirt seem almost slovenly. It was, she realized with a small shock, the first time she'd seen Quinn Eisley in uniform. It was a forceful reminder of who and what he was—a soldier in an ugly war, the four gold stripes on his shoulder boards testimony to how long he'd been fighting it.

John made the introductions as she took a chair at the opposite end of the table, and the briefing she had interrupted resumed. As it progressed, she realized that this was the first the others knew of the theft of the arms and the operation to recover them. She listened in silence, content with being ignored. With the supersonic speed of the little jet and the five-hour time difference between Ireland and Washington, she'd experienced the unique phenomenon of arriving before she'd left, but she still could have used a few more hours' sleep before the telephone had rung. The call requesting her presence at the debriefing had been unexpected, which was why she was late; always before she had reported to John privately. The request was even more of a surprise, Blue thought wryly, because she had assumed that, as of the moment she'd said Quinn Eisley's name, she was "retired." Apparently not. At least, not yet.

"So the operation was a success, but the patient died."

Silently Quinn agreed with Nelson's sour summation of the mission's mixed success. MI5 had identified the dead hijackers as members of an Irish Protestant terrorist organization that periodically traded killings with the IRA. They had prevented a few more bloody stains on Ireland's fabled green; they'd gotten the weapons back and the money, but not what they'd wanted most—the thief.

"You have no idea what number Heaney was talking about?"

Blue looked at the spare, sallow man asking the question. She knew all their names, but it was the first opportunity she'd had to put faces with any of them. Paul Ritterbush was Damage Control's expert in interrogation, which was no doubt why his question to Quinn sounded like one.

"I have an idea," Quinn answered neutrally, dropping a scrap of paper in the middle of the table.

The men leaned forward; then Ritterbush shot him a sharp glance. "Does MI5 know about this?"

He exchanged a glance with John. "No." Even among allies, Blue had discovered, trust was selective.

With a stubby forefinger, John delicately touched the same corner by which Quinn had held the Band-Aid-size scrap and turned it so that the number scrawled on it was right-side up. "Where did you get it?"

"Heaney had it stashed in his sock. The thief undoubtedly told him to destroy the letter, and he must have, because I didn't find it when I searched his flat, but he was probably worried that he'd forget the number, so he wrote it down."

Opinions were offered around the table. "It could be some kind of code." Martin Tiano, a caricature of anonymity, had recently retired from fieldwork and was now in charge of logistics.

"Maybe a locker number and combination." Roy Durbidge, the operations chief, spoke in a raspy whisper, one souvenir of a five-year stay in the Hanoi Hilton.

"Or a phone number." The communications expert was Glenn Kemper, a dark mastiff of a man.

"Or an account number."

A feminine voice was an unfamiliar intrusion in that room, and, like a chorus line, the men's heads snapped toward Blue Harrell. She met their stares, not in aggressive challenge, Quinn saw, but as an equal, establishing her right to speak. "I think you're right," he said, seconding the theory he'd been about to suggest himself.

Involuntarily Blue looked at him, and he inclined his head slightly in silent acknowledgment. To feel the satisfaction she felt was foolish, Blue told herself.

John frowned at the paper again. "You may have something. Let's get the Librarian on it." He picked up the phone by his left elbow, dialed, then spoke after the length of a ring. "Hal, would you come to the conference room?"

Quinn heard the almost imperceptible hesitation before Nelson spoke the man's name, as if he'd had to call it up from memory. He probably had. Damage Control didn't go in for code names; Hal Ladwig was "the Librarian" because his only identity was his job. Like all librarians, his job was information, but instead of books, his facts came from computers. Reputedly there wasn't a system in the world that he couldn't crack nor an electronic brain he couldn't pick, and Quinn had seen evidence of his skill often enough to believe it. While in college, he'd broken into Naval Intelligence's supposedly unbreakable super-computer just to see if he could do it. He'd been caught only because his bargain-basement equipment couldn't keep up with him. Popular opinion had been to lock him up for twenty years, out of reach of even a pocket calculator, but Nelson had offered him a job, instead.

The door opened, and Blue had to fight the urge to smile. Even without John's description, she would have known this was Hal Ladwig. Thin, stoop-shouldered, sandy hair straggling over the collar of his plaid shirt, he was almost too much the classic computer nerd. The only thing missing was tape on his horn-rims.

John handed him the scrap of paper. "See if this is some kind of account number, will you, Hal? Then send it on to the lab for a complete analysis."

"Sure thing." Hal aimed a quick nod at the table in general and left.

"Heaney's death was very convenient," Paul Ritterbush said to no one in particular.

"Not to Heaney." Quinn's dry comment was received with equally dry laughter, yet Blue felt a strengthening of the undercurrent she'd noticed when she'd entered the room. She'd thought that she was the reason, but now she wasn't so sure.

"The autopsy report said the bullets came from one of our HK MP5s. The hijackers didn't have those, did they?" This time Ritterbush slanted a look at Quinn.

Quinn returned it levelly. "No, they didn't."

"Quinn doesn't like killing. He's more into modified disabling." Glenn Kemper's wisecrack got laughs, too, but the undercurrent didn't ease, and Blue knew its source now.

"Captain Eisley didn't shoot Heaney," she said quietly.

"You're certain?" Paul Ritterbush's sharp tone didn't quite mask his disappointment.

Blue gave him a cool look. "I'm certain." Had that been the real reason John had given her the job, one he hadn't bothered to mention? To confirm that Quinn Eisley was honest?

Quinn saw the uncertain frown Blue Harrell shot Nelson. He'd wondered if Nelson had told her to make sure he was still on the right side, along with watching his back. As soon as he'd joined Damage Control, he'd realized that Nelson didn't trust anyone, not even his own men, but from the look, he knew Nelson hadn't told her to check him out, although the result had been the same. The theft had been computer-engineered, from the order to ship the arms as part of a routine surplus weapons sale to one of the United States's NATO partners to the documents that had allowed the weapons to be temporarily stored in a Belfast warehouse. It was possible that a criminal hacker could have masterminded the theft, but the cracker would have had to break into several systems to get all the necessary authorization codes and generate the paperwork, and he would have had to have known about Heaney. It was far more likely that the theft had been engineered by someone inside Naval Intelligence, and Damage Control was as inside as it got. The six men sitting around the table now, along with the Librarian, had the clearance to access the codes and the comparatively rudimentary computer skills to handle the paperwork, and Heaney's dossier was readily available in the Librarian's vast collection. Because of the contacts he had made as O'Rourke, he had to be a prime suspect, but—Quinn glanced at the woman at the end of the table—whether he'd intended it or not, Nelson had provided him with an alibi.

Roy Durbidge asked the logical follow-up question. "Did you see who shot him?"

Blue shook her head. "No. After the first shot, I didn't see him again."

The men moved on to motives for Heaney's death, favoring the obvious one that the IRA had seen a perfect opportunity to get its investment back, and Blue let the discussion go on without her. The undercurrent of suspicion was still there, but no longer focused, she sensed, on Quinn. Technically, she couldn't claim that she was sure he hadn't shot Heaney, because she hadn't watched him every second, but she *knew* it, absolutely. What Glenn Kemper had said was true—Quinn Eisley had no fondness for killing. She'd seen him have the opportunities—and it could certainly be argued the justification—but he hadn't taken them. Violence was a fact of his life, and he wasn't afraid of it. His strong survival instincts and superior physical skills and intelligence had been honed with intensive training and even harsher experience until he handled violence with a frighteningly calm assurance, but he hadn't developed a liking for it. She had no doubt that he had killed, but he didn't do it casually.

The door opened again, and Hal Ladwig came in with a computer printout in his hand. He pushed at the bridge of his glasses before he spoke. A nervous habit, Blue concluded, since they didn't seem to be sliding down his thin nose. "It's a bank account number. The account was opened by Universal Exports at the Manhattan branch of the Otsuki Bank a little over three weeks ago. There's a branch in Belfast, too."

"Same time as the theft," Glenn Kemper murmured, and several of the other men nodded, acknowledging the significance of the dates and branch locations.

"It was opened with ten thousand dollars, cash, and there's been no activity in the account since." Hal glanced up from the printout. "I ran the address for the company. It doesn't exist, and Universal Exports isn't listed anywhere that I've found so far."

Quinn considered the scant information. "Can you tell if the account was opened in person, or did someone break into the bank's computer and add it in?"

"The account record says in person, but that doesn't prove anything. The only way to know for sure is to see if the bank branch has paperwork with an actual signature."

Roy Durbidge reached for the printout. "I'll send someone up to New York to find out."

Nelson approved of Durbidge's plan with a nod, then looked back to the Librarian. "Still no luck backtracking the thief?"

Ladwig and an assistant had begun searching for electronic fingerprints as soon as the theft was discovered. "Sterba and I are still working on it, but—" he shrugged "—nothing so far. Whoever this guy is, he knows computers," he added in a tone that was as much admiring as grudging.

"Well, keep at it." Nelson stood up, signaling that the meeting was over. As the men and Blue Harrell rose from their chairs and started for the door, Quinn saw the subtle maneuvering. The Librarian, he thought cynically, was more man than microchip after all, but it was Nelson who walked out with her. They disappeared into his office, and Quinn stared at the closed door for a second or two before going in the opposite direction. Passing the desk of Damage Control's head secretary, he stopped suddenly.

"What's the name of that, Lieutenant?"

The lieutenant looked up warily. The first time she had seen Quinn Eisley, he'd literally taken her breath away. Men like him didn't come the way of an average mortal woman every day, sometimes not even once in a lifetime, but a second look at those cold, dead eyes and she'd lost any thoughts of trying to lure them her way. She looked in the direction he was pointing and carefully masked her surprise. She would never, in her wildest daydreams, have imagined him to be interested in flowers. "Lobelia, sir," she said.

A long lean finger reached out to touch one of the tiny, deep blue flowers growing in the pot on the corner of her desk before he turned away abruptly. Mystified, she watched him walk down the hall to his office.

Blue glanced down the escalator behind her, then across to the one moving in the opposite direction to the subway station below. A class of five- or six-year-olds was going back to school after a field trip to the zoo, and her eyes lingered on a small red-haired boy with bright blue eyes. The pain came, no longer a jagged tearing slash, but now a dull ache, heart deep.

The children passed by, and she stared at the empty steps and blank walls ahead. The Metro had to dive deep under Rock Creek, putting the station so far down that at midpoint on the long escalators linking the underground to the surface, neither the ending or beginning of the moving stairways was visible, creating the eerie illusion of a never-ending ride to nowhere. Finally the treads flattened and disappeared under the tile floor. Blue crossed the short landing to a second escalator because, despite being as long as was technically possible, the first still wasn't long enough to reach the surface, and she started moving upward through the blank emptiness again.

Stepping off the last step into the strong afternoon sunshine brought the peculiar sense of completing a long wearisome journey. Ten minutes later she opened the door of her apartment and stepped inside. She paused, then, more with a sense of inevitability than surprise, closed the door behind her.

"You're lucky I didn't shoot you," Quinn Eisley said conversationally.

He was continuing the conversation that she'd so rudely interrupted two days ago by passing out. Even that didn't surprise her; she'd already known that he didn't believe in polite preliminaries, and that she wouldn't escape a reckoning. A corner of her mouth turned down wryly. "Before or after you found out who I was?"

His laughter was deep and genuinely free, and splinters of it seemed to penetrate her, creating an odd, purling warmth. "Both." He was out of uniform, wearing dark jeans, well-worn leather sneakers and a black T-shirt that pulled tight over his shoulders and flat stomach as he stood up from her small dining table. "I owe you—twice."

It was more thanks than she had expected. "Actually," she slanted him a look as she laid her leather satchel on the worktable near the door, "you owe me three times."

Blue saw the mental finger snap as his eyes abruptly narrowed, but she sensed it was confirmation of a suspicion, not surprise. "Marrakech. The kid on the motorbike."

As he'd thought, she had been the dark-haired "boy" in the cap and dirty jellaba who had come racing through the old market on a motorbike and clipped a stall of watermelons, sending them rolling and exploding across the narrow street. The last he'd seen of the two Libyans stalking him, they were sprawled in the dirt, soaking up juice and screaming curses after the speeding kid.

She sketched a self-mocking bow, then asked, with another sideways look, "Just out of curiosity, I've always wondered how you had planned to get away from the three on Cyprus."

"The same way you did—bump somebody's drinking arm, wait till the fight got going good, then run like hell—only I'd picked the table of French sailors." A grin played around the edges of his mouth. "They were closer to the door, and drunker."

She didn't smile in return. "But you didn't run. You waited. Why?"

"You'd done me a favor unknowingly—or so I thought at the time," he added dryly. "I wanted to make sure you were—" his face became expressionless "—safe."

Safe? Blue almost laughed out loud. Safe was the last thing she was, especially with him. She no longer woke up in the middle of the night, terrified of something she couldn't see, only feel—an absolute aloneness. She no longer existed in a daze, not happy, not sad, not anything, dead to all feeling. She had gone through the period of just surviving: eating, breathing, filling her time but not really living. She was living now. She was working and enjoying it. She'd reactivated old friendships, made new ones. She was living, not alive yet, but living, and she wasn't ready for more. She didn't want to be tempted to look for more, to need, to want. And he tempted.

Quinn watched her cross to the tall windows on the other side of the room as if she were suddenly restless. She was wearing khaki pants and an open-necked blue work shirt with the sleeves turned back, and the late-afternoon sun burning through the windows highlighted her hair and shone through the loose shirt, limning the straight line of her ribs and the rounded curve of one breast. After a moment he shifted to the view out the window. He finally knew what color her hair was, he thought absently; it was black. He stared at the roofline across the street. He'd fought a battle with himself for two days. What Nelson had told him about her hadn't satisfied his curiosity; it had only intensified it until curiosity had become near-obsession, and he'd lost the battle. She had invaded his privacy, been his intimate shadow for months, yet he knew next to nothing about her. He needed to know everything, to see where she lived, to see how she occupied herself when she wasn't with him, to see . . . her.

"Why did you take the job?" He'd wondered if it was simply that she had needed the money, but now that he saw where she lived and the stained-glass pieces on the worktable and stacked against the walls, he knew money wasn't the reason. The loft apartment was essentially one large workroom, its primary function stated in the wide wooden worktable that ran nearly the length of it. The oak floor and white walls were bare, and furniture was minimal, not cheap, but obviously chosen for utility, not aesthetics. There was an efficient kitchenette in one corner and an equally efficent bathroom behind the one interior door. The only bed was a single, neatly made and covered with a plain white spread.

"John needed someone, and I had the background and the time," she answered readily.

Her reason was the same as Nelson's, and, just like his, not the real one. A stained-glass window lay on the worktable like a partially completed jigsaw puzzle, the rest of the pieces scattered around it. Like the woman herself, Quinn thought. He was here to put together more pieces of the puzzle of Blue Harrell. Picking up a diamond of green opalescent glass, he idly examined it. "You've known Nelson a long time."

"As long as I can remember. He and my parents were friends for years. In fact, John was the one who arranged my adoption."

She waited in silence, uncertain of what he wanted. He seemed to have nothing more on his mind than the pieces of colored glass he was picking up and setting down, yet from the moment she'd entered the apartment, the atmosphere had seemed sexually charged and more than a little dangerous. Like the man himself, she reminded herself. Abruptly she turned back to the satchel she'd left on the worktable and began to pull out the contents.

Nelson had arranged her adoption. That was a detail he'd left out. Quinn turned a completed roundel of a brilliant gold sunburst in his hands. "This is beautiful work."

She heard the inherent compliment. "It is beautiful, but I didn't make it. I just repaired it," she said briefly.

He laid the small masterpiece back on the worktable. "Without your repair, it would just be another broken window."

"Perhaps."

Her noncommittal shrug was accompanied by a small smile. She aligned a soldering iron with several others on an asbestos pad, then pulled a spool of copper ribbon out of the satchel and a roll of grooved metal strip that he guessed was the leading that held panes of glass together. "Were you out on a repair job this afternoon?"

Blue set the spool of copper foil beside one of soldering flux and hung the lead on a dowel above the bench. "A minor one at the Ford Theatre. Just a broken pane."

"You fixed it there?"

She saw him glance at the numerous pieces around the room awaiting repair. "Minor damage I can usually fix on-site. When the damage is more extensive, it's easier to do the work here." She picked up the roundel he'd set down a minute before. The glass was still warm from his hands, and her fingers greedily sought the warmth, absorbing it. "This and those over there—" she indicated a row of large panels encased in heavy protective frames "—belong to a church in Lynchburg, Virginia. Their windows are appraised at a million dollars." She grimaced ruefully. "I've got about two hundred thousand dollars' worth of them here."

Quinn frowned at the smashed panes and dangling lead strips that made the parts still intact that much more beautiful and the damage that much more tragic. "Why didn't the church have some kind of protection over them?"

"They did, but Plexiglas isn't much protection against a tornado." He was leaning against the worktable, a scant arm's length away, his eyes intent on her, not the windows. To redirect them, she waved a hand toward several yellowed sheets of drawings pinned to the tack strip behind the worktable. "Fortunately, the church has the artist's original drawings, which makes things much easier for me."

Quinn laughed harshly to himself. "Things" weren't any easier for him. He was still trying to find the answer to the question he'd first asked himself two days ago. *Who was she?* It was almost impossible to reconcile the woman standing in front of him now, in clean sunlight, surrounded by the beauty she preserved, with the woman who had knelt in dirt and blood in a dark warehouse, surrounded by ugliness and death. Yet the two were one in the same.

It hadn't been hard to access her file in the District of Columbia's police department records. Going through official channels was time-consuming and inconvenient, especially when Damage Control didn't officially exist, so shortcuts were routine. Nelson hadn't given a reason for her transfer to the Justice Department, but he'd found it. Like many rookies, her first assignment had been undercover, and she'd proved particularly adept at it, staying with it until her fatal "flaw" was discovered. She hadn't hesitated to defend another's life, but when her own was threatened, she had. That incident and the subsequent psychological profiling had shown that Blue Harrell would immediately act to protect someone else, but she would hesitate that deadly fraction of a second to protect herself, so, to safeguard her, a transfer was arranged to the Justice Department. She had worked as an investigator in the Terrorism and Violent Crimes Division, still dealing with ugliness and death on a daily basis, but out of harm's way.

The anger he had felt when he understood just what Nelson had done still burned, hotter now that he saw the other half of her life—what the whole of her life should be. Nelson had put her back in harm's way, callously taking advantage of her "flaw" by making her responsible for his life, no doubt suspecting that she felt she had failed to save her family, so she would try that much harder to save him. The bastard.

"How did you get interested in restoration?"

Wondering at the undertone of anger in the question, Blue dealt leftover glass scraps into their respective bins at the back of the table. "You mean—" she gave him a small ironic grin "—how did I go from sneaking and snooping to soldering and glass cutting?" John would have told him her background; Eisley would have demanded it. "While I was living in Paris a few years ago, the church down the street started restoring its antique windows. I'd worked with stained glass as a hobby, and one day I stopped to talk to the workmen. The next thing I knew—" her shoulders lifted in a helpless shrug as she laughed ''—I had a new career.''

She would have had no trouble talking to the workmen; French had been her first language, and her file said she had retained her fluency, along with the Arabic she'd learned in Tangiers when she was a little girl. He regarded her small body lazily. She was still a ''little girl.''

His grin was more fully formed this time, reminding her of still another danger, yet Blue found herself sitting across from him at the dining table a few minutes later, not certain which of them had initiated the move. He looked at the restored rose window that she'd hung against one of the outside windows so that she could enjoy the sun-blazoned kaleidoscope of colors before the owner came to take it away. ''Is that some of your own work?''

''I repair. I don't create.''

Anymore. She didn't have to say it, but it was there, and it didn't take any intelligence to figure out when she had stopped creating her own pieces. Talking about the glass, she had come alive. Now, with the wrong question, she had lapsed back into the flat, almost robotic manner he'd seen in Belfast. It was even more maddening now.

''You have a good place to work,'' he said with a look around the loft.

Grateful that he wasn't interested in pursuing the previous topic, Blue answered quickly. ''John found it for me and helped me get everything set up.''

He fought to keep the incredulous look off his face. Nelson apartment hunting and shopping for furniture was almost impossible to picture. "It must be hard to find the glass you need. Do you buy old windows and take them apart?"

"Sometimes, but new glass is available to match most of the old." Animation returned to her voice as she gestured toward a large restored panel leaning against one of the windows. Backlit by the lowering sun, the red and orange and yellow glass flames leapt to vivid life. "That's a Tiffany window, over a hundred years old. A third of the glass in it is new, although you can't tell it. The glass company in Indiana that supplied Tiffany and a number of other artists is still in business, still using the same formulas, so I can often order exactly what I need."

"Why did you take the job?"

She should have known the first time he asked the question that he'd accepted her answer too easily, Blue thought. Her reaction was instinctive—to put some distance between them while she considered her next answer, but she'd forgotten how fast he could move. Her chair had hardly begun to slide back when his foot jammed behind one leg, locking her in place. Blue met his eyes and knew the only answer was the truth. "I wanted to protect you," she said tonelessly.

Even though he had anticipated her answer, it still jarred him, and Quinn felt no satisfaction at having his suspicions of Nelson's brutal callousness confirmed. He'd operated alone for so many years, that the concept of anyone protecting him was almost unbelievable, especially when his protector wasn't doing it because she was ordered to, but because she wanted to.

She pushed against the edge of the table again, and he let her up this time. "You'll have to excuse me now, Quinn," she said with perfect courtesy as she moved to the door. "I promised a window for tomorrow, and I haven't finished it."

She was the robot again, and suddenly he was determined to crack that emotionless facade, to provoke some kind of reaction out of her, to give her a taste of what she provoked in him. Anger, frustration, guilt—he felt a confusion of emotions he hadn't felt in years, maybe never . . . and never because of a woman. But there was one emotion that wasn't confused: basic, unalloyed desire.

Blue breathed a silent sigh when he stood up. She wanted him gone, before he asked the next "why"— why had she wanted to protect him? It was a question for which she had no answer . . . or maybe too many answers, all of them too disturbing to deal with right now.

As she reached to open the door, he moved again. He said nothing, simply locked his fist in her hair to keep her head back as his mouth came down on hers. The floor suddenly listed, and she staggered, without moving. Her arms limp at her sides, she just stood there, making no attempt to pull free as, hard and hungry, his mouth took hers with ruthless expertise. She gave him what he wanted, what *she* wanted, unable—in truth, unwilling—to do anything else. The fist wound in her hair kept her mouth tight to his while his other hand curved around her throat, his thumb under her chin, tilting her head, perfecting the angle.

His tongue slid over hers, and she tasted hot desire and sharp pleasure, and abruptly the kiss was too much.

She jerked her mouth free. His hand still tight in her hair, he let her move a scant inch away. Something flickered in his eyes, too brief to be identified. Then his fist loosened and his hand slowly slid free, as if he were letting her hair trail between his fingers to test the fineness, savor the silkiness, of it. He smiled faintly as his hand dropped away and he stepped back. "We both have something to finish, Blue."

As the door closed behind him, Blue went to the light table, snapped it on and positioned a piece of bull's-eye glass over the illuminated drawing already in place. She picked up a marker and, with studied care, began transferring the pattern on the paper to the glass.

Without warning, the marker slid out of her fingers, rolling off the table and across the floor as her sham of indifference came to an abrupt end. She felt scorched. Slowly she straightened, one hand closing into a fist to press against the still heavy throb in her chest as she turned to stare at the blank door. Closing her eyes, she drew a ragged breath.

God help her, she was alive.

Chapter 6

Scrubbing sweat off his face and neck, Quinn started for the locker room. As he slung the towel into a canvas hamper, he saw who was leaning against the railing, watching the action in one of the handball courts below, and changed direction.

Nelson glanced up as he stood beside him. "Full contact?"

Quinn grunted as he stripped off the thin pads he'd worn during the karate session.

Nelson shook his head with a short laugh. "That's one aspect of fieldwork I don't miss."

Curious to see what Nelson found so fascinating, Quinn glanced below, then back again for a longer look. A dozen women in workout clothes sat on the mat-covered floor, intent on the stocky red-haired man and dark-haired woman in T-shirts and gym pants in front of them, their backs to the watchers above. "When did Blue become one of the instructors?"

"She didn't. Macklin oversaw her physical training when she was preparing for you. She took both of his courses as a tune-up, and occasionally he asks her to fill in when one of the regular instructors can't make it." Sparing him a sardonic glance, Nelson answered his next question before he could ask it. "You never saw her because you were still watching the hole in your chest heal up."

Macklin's voice came from below. "Remember, any time you touch an attacker, you're giving him something to break off." Macklin demonstrated, lunging toward Blue. She reached out an arm to ward him off, conveying a sense of pleading helplessness. Macklin grabbed her arm and twisted, leaving their audience in no doubt that he could snap it if he wanted to.

"How was Bahamas?" Quinn asked without looking at the man beside him.

"A waste of time. I don't know why the hell that bank clerk had to pick this week for her vacation. Garcia had to traipse all over the damn island to track her down for me."

"Rough duty," Quinn murmured dryly, still studying the action below. Releasing Blue's arm, Macklin steadied her with an easy hand on her shoulder. The sudden violence Quinn felt at the sight of Macklin touching her lingered far longer than Macklin's hand.

"The clerk couldn't give a description of the P. K. Walther who opened the Universal Exports account. Not that she could be expected to," Nelson conceded grudgingly, "after a month. At least she did remember it was a man, confirming the lab's handwriting analysis that the writer was male, using the wrong hand. All she remembered about him was that he was wearing a hat and coat and gloves like everyone else that day because of the blizzard, which explains why we only have her fingerprints and the file clerk's on the card. He waited for lousy weather when people would have thought it was odd if he *wasn't* wearing gloves.''

To the accompaniment of the women's nervous laughter, Macklin assured them that they could deal with an attacker so that anything that got broken would be his. Macklin didn't, Quinn knew, allow a woman to think she was invincible, since the course trained a woman to deal with a single, unarmed attacker. His goal was to give a woman the confidence to help herself in a threatening situation. An ex-SEAL, Macklin was an eighth-degree black belt in karate and a master of kick boxing and Japanese fencing, but what he taught the women in his self-defense classes was basic dirty fighting. He didn't teach them how to dance, Quinn thought with grim approval; he taught them how to fight for their lives. "Did the bank clerk recognize anyone from the photos?" he asked casually.

He'd expected Nelson's sharp look although he didn't acknowledge it. Normal procedure would have been for Ritterbush to send a man to interview the bank clerk. The fact that Nelson had taken on the job personally could only mean that he had wanted to ask or show the clerk something that he didn't trust anyone else to, and Quinn was certain it was something he'd wanted to show her—photographs of Ritterbush, Tiano, Durbidge, Kemper, the Librarian, Sterba ... and himself.

"No," Nelson said after a minute.

Macklin held up shin guards, elbow and knee pads, padded body armor and a foam-covered Fiberglas beehive helmet with mesh-protected eye and mouth holes, as he explained to the women that he would be wearing the protection when he "mugged" them. The thirty pounds of padding and helmet weren't just to protect Macklin but also to overcome the women's natural inhibitions against hurting someone. A woman earned her graduation when she dealt Macklin what would be a knockout blow to an assailant.

Macklin explained exactly how he was going to attack them so the women had no illusions that they were playing, warning that he would knock them down and force them to fight on their backs because that was how rape victims usually ended up. Having seen him in action a few times, Quinn knew he wasn't talking just for effect. Macklin attacked with full power to provoke the adrenaline rush that came with fear, forcing the women to cope with rubbery knees and frozen muscles, to push them past the initial terror response and condition them to react instinctively to protect themselves. It was imperative, he reminded them, that they take action to disable an assailant immediately and not waste their strength on useless struggling. Nelson said Blue had taken this course and Macklin's advanced one in handling armed and multiple assailants. He wondered if Macklin had been successful in helping her to overcome that lethal split second of hesitation before defending herself.

After telling the class that he and Blue were now going to give them a demonstration of what he'd been talking about, Macklin picked up the protective gear and started for the locker room to put it on.

"You know, even with all that protection, he's been knocked out twice and gotten a couple of cracked ribs," Nelson began, then realized he was talking to himself.

Slipping on pads that would protect her forearms and hands, Blue glanced at the walls of the court, scuffed from the years of hard rubber balls bouncing off them. With no juice bar, no up-to-the-minute exercise fads and no quasi-singles bar atmosphere, Hanson's could make no pretense of being a "health club." It was an unapologetically old-fashioned gym, and Blue appreciated it. All male until a few years before, the membership was still mostly men who were polite and friendly without being obnoxiously so, although a few of the older ones, she thought as the door in the rear wall opened, occasionally looked a little bemused, as if they still couldn't quite understand how women had breached their masculine domain.

Wearing worn overalls and a football jersey that bulged grotesquely with padding, black castlike pads over his palms and forearms, and a helmet resembling a giant hornet's nest, the man inside the mugger getup lost his identity, making his nightmarish figure even more threatening. The women settled themselves quickly on the mats, instinctively moving closer together as he approached. Posture wasn't the usual thing to notice about a man, Blue supposed. Quinn Eisley's was perfect, not the military school stiff-spined standard, but a much rarer, natural, perfect alignment and coordination of each body part with every other so that he moved with an elegance of strength, harmony and fluidity—even when he looked like something from a teenage slasher movie.

Following Macklin's script, Quinn suddenly lunged to catch Blue off guard, as a victim would be. Before he could seize her, her foot lashed out and up with a precise aim that made him very grateful for the most heavily fortified part of the costume. Life as a eunuch had little appeal.

She'd overcome her reluctance to defend herself, he thought sardonically, backing out of range and holding up one hand to indicate that a disabling blow had been landed. Circling, he feinted to the left, and she went to the right, not falling for the ploy, so he simply rushed her. It was her knee that made him grateful for the protection this time as his hand went up again.

Gasping for breath, Blue backed away. It was incredible how fast and how suddenly he moved, even more incredible considering the heavy, awkward padding and helmet. Deliberately she turned her back on him and walked away, her muscles tensing in anticipation of his next attack. It came without even the whispered warning of his padded boots on the mat behind her. His long arms snaked around her, jerking her off her feet, yet, oddly, she didn't feel the momentary instinctual panic she always did when Terry Macklin did this.

His arms crossed over her chest, Quinn caught himself regretting the thick padding on his arms. Her heel connected solidly with his shin, then her other foot stomped down on his instep, snapping him back to attention and reminding him to be thankful that she was wearing sneakers, not spiked heels. He was debating whether the combination counted as a crippling blow when she went limp, her head falling forward, then just as suddenly snapping back to clip the chin of the helmet with enough force to settle the debate, and his hand went up a third time.

Their audience had been watching in seemingly stunned silence, but with the head shot, they came alive with a loud cheer. Not giving her time to get set for his next attack, he charged and pushed her to the mat, but she recovered even as she was falling. More by accident than any skill of his own, he dodged the sharp, slashing elbow aimed at his throat.

"Bite!" The watching women began shouting enthusiastic advice. "Kick him! Eyes! Go for his eyes!"

She was doing her best to follow the women's instructions, Quinn thought dryly as he jerked his head out of range of her stabbing fingers while parrying that persistent knee. He gained control by sheer brute force, and it took more than he had wanted to use against her. Her strength astounded him. Without the graphic demonstration, he never would have believed such a small, slight body could pack so much punch.

He stared down at her, pinned and seemingly helpless, yet with a look of unholy delight in her eyes, and, for a moment, he wondered if she'd guessed who he was. Just as fast he discounted the possibility. No one could have told her about the switch, and, although Macklin was watching, she'd never looked up to see him standing next to Nelson. She couldn't see the color of his eyes through the mesh, and Macklin and he were close enough to the same height that she couldn't tell the difference. Macklin was stockier, but the pads hid that difference, too. There was no way she could have recognized him.

She flexed an arm experimentally against his hold, and his eyes followed the movement. Her skin was flushed a delicate rose and looked so soft, belying the hard muscle underneath. The loud voices of the women watching seemed to recede as her arm flexed again, and the sleeve of her T-shirt rode up, exposing the vulnerable, even softer-looking underside of her arm. He saw the marks then, and unconsciously his fingers eased their grip.

It was all she needed. Wrenching her arm free, she swung up her balled fist in a classic volleyball serve that caught him perfectly under the chin. Yellow stars danced in front of his eyes as his teeth snapped together and his head rocked back. This time there was no debate. Releasing her, Quinn rolled onto his back and held up both hands, the signal that he'd received a knockout blow, and surrendered.

The cheers of the class rang in his ears as Blue reached down a hand to help him up, and, with a still-disbelieving laugh, he took it. "Thank you," she said in a grave voice that went no farther than his ears, "for the demonstration—Quinn."

* * *

Ignoring the cruising cab that slowed down in hope of a fare, Blue swung her tote bag over her shoulder. Minutes before, she had refused John's offer of a ride, too, sensing that although the offer was sincere, he was anxious to return to his office and the frustrating puzzle of the armory theft. Besides, it was still early, the evening was perfect for a walk, and a Metro station was only three blocks away.

She had gone one of those blocks when a car drove past her, slowing, then pulled up to the curb, and the passenger door opened.

"I'll take you home."

As they had been a week—only a week?—before in another dark car, the first thing she saw were his eyes, but this time she saw something in them, something that had her pulling the door open wider and sliding onto the seat instead of closing it in flat refusal. The words were spoken with the usual arrogant certainty that she would comply, but in his eyes she'd glimpsed a request, not a demand. He drove as she would have expected: competent, sure and a little fast. The sedan was dark, heavy and powerful, like so many of the cars in D.C. that she had once wondered half-seriously if they were a requirement of residence, like power ties and Coach handbags. The car was, she thought, studying his shadow-etched features as he glanced over at her, his only chance for anonymity.

"Don't you have a car?"

"I have one, but parking in Washington is impossible. It's easier to take the Metro." He was back in uniform, but his hair was still damp from the quick

shower he must have taken, curling against his neck
and over his ears.

Out of habit, Quinn checked the rearview mirror.
She was right; it was easier, and with ever-present
uniformed transit cops and more in plainclothes, it
was at least as safe as the cab she'd passed up, but he
still didn't like the idea of her riding in it after dark.
And he wasn't sure he liked the fact that he didn't like
it.

Lulled by the smooth motion of the car and the peculiarly comfortable silence between them, Blue sat
back and just enjoyed the ride. A brief shower had left
the street wet, and the head and taillights of the moving traffic turned it into a shining silver ribbon strung
with glittering diamonds and rubies. She watched the
windows of the city light up one by one for blocks before noticing where they were going. Slowly she turned
to look at him. "I guess I should have asked whose
home."

His mouth curved up as he continued to look
straight ahead. "Yeah."

With a soft laugh, Blue relaxed back against the
seat. Somewhere deep in her gene pool, she thought
with a silent, half-despairing laugh, there must have
been a moth who had thought she was flameproof.

She had been expecting an apartment in a downtown high rise off the Beltway, not a Federal-period
town house in Georgetown on a narrow street watched
over by magnificent old oaks. The inside was yet another surprise. The house had been modernized, of
course, but the original fireplace, woodwork and oak

floor and staircase had been preserved. In the living room there were a long, comfortable-looking leather sofa and matching easy chairs, and an array of sophisticated electronics. One of the pillows was pushed up against an arm of the couch, a head-size dent in it, and an open book lay on top of a pair of sneakers on the floor beside it. A picture of him lying on the couch reading, then falling asleep, came without warning and with perfect clarity. The image of him doing something so natural and ordinary was somehow too intimate, and she looked away.

The old and the new harmonized like the gem colors worn soft in the Oriental carpet on the polished floor. No decorator had designed the comfort and welcoming she felt here, Blue thought with a sudden constriction in her chest. He had a *home,* not empty white space.

"Would you like something to drink?"

"No, thank you," she murmured, glancing up the staircase and imagining the layout of the bedrooms above.

She turned at the touch on her arm. She hadn't heard him move. Because he was lean muscle rather than heavy bulk, she sometimes forgot how big he was, but seeing him towering over her now, his shoulders blocking out the overhead light, it refreshed her memory. Wordlessly, he pushed up the short sleeve of her shirt, and abruptly Blue knew what had caused him to ease his hold on her, giving her an opportunity she could never have realistically expected to have. The imprint of his fingers and thumb had faded from brilliant blue to a muddy yellow-purple, but the bruises were still clear. His expression unreadable, his attention shifted to the faded bruise on her cheek, his thumb whispering a caress over the faint mark.

"Where else?"

"My shoulder, my side and my hip, my thigh." With an effort, Blue matched his even tone.

She was still looking up at him when he unbuttoned the first button of her shirt. She couldn't help the small startled flinch but she stood still, sensing that his need to see the damage for himself was stronger — just — than her certainty that allowing him to touch her wasn't wise. He unbuttoned the second button and the third, then shifted the fabric, and Blue concentrated on the thin white line that appeared around his taut mouth, not the slightly raspy fingertips feathering over her shoulder and upper arm, or the radiating shivers of heat that followed them.

The stark contrast between the white strap of her bra and the vivid green and yellow and purple mottling the skin underneath twisted the knife in his gut a little deeper. Her blouse was butter-soft silk, and her skin was even softer, as he'd imagined . . . Abruptly Quinn squatted in front of her and pulled the blouse free of the waistband of the long full skirt she wore and hiked up the tail. The bruising on her ribs was the same as that on her shoulder, with the added extra of a darker welt that no doubt matched one of the ribs of the oil barrel he'd slammed her against.

Lowering his hands to the hem of her skirt, he began raising it, pausing at the scars. He'd known they would be there — she couldn't have crawled through broken glass and hot cinders and not had them — but they were no worse than the ones on her hands. He continued up to the massive bruise on the outside of her thigh, bunching her skirt in one fist so he could turn her leg to appreciate the full extent of the ugly discoloration. The skin of her inner thigh against his palm was silkier than her shoulder.

As her skirt and his palm started to slide higher, Blue stepped away from him. "You'll have to take my word about the one on my hip," she said, striving for a lightness she didn't feel as she rebuttoned her shirt. The suppressed anger she had sensed in him as soon as he'd touched her hadn't diminished, and, although she knew it wasn't directed at her, she wanted it gone for several reasons—not the least of which was that she needed nothing that heightened her awareness of him. She was beginning to be able to see past his guarded emptiness, and the realization truly frightened her.

There was no sign of lightness in his hard expression as he stood up. "I didn't know it was you." Quinn clamped his mouth shut. He was offering her an explanation, and he wasn't in the habit of justifying himself.

A purist wouldn't call it an apology, but then, Quinn Eisley, she was certain, had little practice making them, or feeling the need to. To cover a sudden feeling of vulnerability, Blue dismissed the bruises with a brisk shrug. "A hazard of the job. Besides," she added with a tiny smile, "I got even tonight."

A corner of his mouth turned up as he rubbed his chin. "Yeah." She didn't blame him, which only made him feel it more. "How did you know it was me?"

"It's been my job to know you, even in a bad Halloween costume." Blue congratulated herself on achieving the proper lightness this time.

It was another of those damned nonanswers she was so good at. He wouldn't have recognized himself in that getup yet, somehow, she had. Quinn gave the cellular phone on the coffee table an impatient glance as it began buzzing. That kind of recognition was instinctual, the kind between a man and a woman who knew each other intimately physically, the kind of primal knowledge that came from sex—long and hot and frequent, until each knew all the secrets of the other's body. The kind that didn't come from a "job." Muttering a terse expletive under his breath, he grabbed the phone. He didn't know how, but she *knew* him.

To give him privacy, Blue moved into the dining ell off the living room. From the subtle tone of respect in his voice, she guessed the person on the other end of the line was John Nelson. When the phone had begun buzzing, she had wondered briefly if it might be a woman, but briefly was all she had permitted herself to wonder. Succumbing to a different curiosity, she pushed open a door to find a bare-bones kitchen, then laughed softly at the contrary satisfaction she felt. Discovering that he was a gourmet cook on top of everything else would have been too much.

She looked back to see that he was still on the phone, frowning, concentrating on the conversation, yet his eyes were focused on her, following her. In response to her questioning glance toward the door open to the hallway, he nodded.

The first door across the hall led into a study. Another Oriental carpet covered the floor, along with two wing chairs, all worn to the point of character. There was another, smaller fireplace, well used, a massive rolltop desk with a compact computer and printer, and a floor-to-ceiling bookcase that took up one wall. The shelves held an eclectic mix of books—novels, nonfiction and, surprisingly, several volumes of poetry, other items and a few photographs.

She touched the brass frame as if it were something fragile and priceless; then her hand moved on to caress another frame, holding it for a long minute. Watching from the doorway, Quinn felt something tear deep inside him. Finally he understood just how much she had lost in the fire three years before. She had been left utterly alone and with absolutely nothing. Orphaned, adopted, then orphaned again, she had no connection to the past and, with the loss of her son, none to the future, the continuum of her life broken. The fire hadn't only taken her son and husband, it had taken every reminder of them, and of her childhood and her parents, as well. Nothing, no childhood keepsakes, no memento of her son, not even one precious photograph, had survived. Her life had burned up, too.

Yet, as she studied each photograph in turn, he didn't see the pain or grief he expected. She was smiling, her eyes soft. When she came to the photograph beside a pair of rusty military ID tags, the smile faded, but the softness remained.

As he moved from the doorway to stand beside her, she glanced up. "Your brother," she said, and he nodded.

Picking up one of the dog tags, she read the name. "Michael," she murmured, then looked back to him. "John said you led the commando team that found the cache of identifications for so many of the Vietnam MIAs, and that your brother's was one of them."

"It was," he confirmed. He'd wondered how much Nelson had told her about him. Quite a bit, apparently.

Nodding, she laid the tag back on the shelf carefully, then looked up to a photograph on the next shelf. "He's one of you, isn't he?" she said, her eyes still on the picture.

"He was. He's retired now." Quinn looked at her curiously. "How did you know?" Nelson would have had no reason to tell her about Dekker.

"You have the same look—always on guard, always ready to move." She glanced from the picture to him and back again. "Dangerous."

He smiled faintly. "His wife says the same thing."

Superficially, the man in the photograph bore little resemblance to the man standing beside her. Blunt-featured, he was as blond as Quinn was dark, possibly a little taller and definitely broader. The woman beside him was blond and tall, too, but almost dwarfed by her husband. They wore shorts and T-shirts, the towheaded child between them wore a swimsuit; and in the background she could see waves breaking on a sand beach. The camera had caught the man and woman looking at each other, a look so intimate, so intensely connected, that Blue almost felt like a voyeur. "His wife looks familiar," she murmured, her throat oddly tight.

"She's Dr. Erin Mathias-Dekker. She—"

"—decoded the whale language," Blue finished in pleased surprise. She picked up the picture to study it more closely. "How old is their little girl?"

"Almost four." He was still watching for pain or sadness or possibly bitter envy, but even now, with the picture of someone else's child, someone else's happy family, he saw, to his peculiarly intense satisfaction, only another smile. "Chloe's the first human to grow up fluent in the language of two species."

Her amazed grin lit her eyes, intensifying the blue until it seemed to glow with a power of its own, a power that caught him and held him captive. She asked another question, and he answered automatically. The warm still air in the study was scented with a clean sweetness. Her scent. It had risen, warm and taunting, from her body as he'd been examining the bruises, enveloping him until all he'd wanted was to bury his nose in the delicate hollow between her neck and her shoulder and drown in it, taste the light sheen of moisture pearlizing her skin ... like the faint sheen he saw now in the shallow valley just visible in the vee of her shirt. He cursed silently as the prowling hunger he had been living with for a week unsheathed its claws, swiping raw desire through him.

Something pierced the habitual cool remoteness in his eyes for a second, too fast for her to identify, but the cauterizing intensity of whatever it was sent a subtle heat through her. As she replaced the photograph, her glance touched each one again: the blond, sun-gilded Dekkers; Quinn and his brother—him in a midshipman's uniform, Michael wearing a flight suit—grinning for the camera and looking impossibly young; an older couple who were clearly his mother and father, both strikingly attractive; and the last, a faded black-and-white of an elderly, ramrod-straight woman. The family resemblance was strong down through the generations. The old eyes looking straight into the camera, she knew instinctively, had been gray.

Did he know what a priceless possession he had in knowing where he had come from, who he had come from? No, of course, he didn't. How could he? Only one who didn't know where she came from, what her roots were, could understand.

Ever since she had first learned what the word adoption meant and how it applied to her, she had felt the lack of hers. It wasn't that her adoptive parents hadn't been good; no "natural" parents could have loved and cared for her more, she knew with complete certainty and gratitude. Yet still the lack was there, no matter how hard she tried to ignore it or tell herself how foolish it was. She had been a foundling with no history, no roots, not even a name to link her to her past, so a part of her was permanently lost. To build a link with her parents that didn't exist in blood, she had chosen the same profession as her father. It had given her the illusion of roots until she matured enough to admit that the illusion was not worth the reality of work for which she didn't have the necessary strength and...hardness. When the offer from the Justice Department had come, she hadn't needed

John's and her parents' encouragement to take it. By the time she had married Paul, she had gained the additional self-knowledge to realize that, while she was good at her work, she didn't want to deal with violence and death and human inhumanity even at arm's length. It had been surprisingly easy to quit, perhaps, in part, because with Paul and then Ben, she had grown roots, to the future if not the past, and didn't need the false roots of her work any longer.

Then those roots had been brutally and irrevocably ripped out, along with any trace of their existence. Even more of her was lost now, yet that didn't explain why she had accepted John's request to return as easily as she had once left. She didn't have the necessary strength and hardness now any more than she had had before, and no roots would magically grow. It wasn't the work this time; it was, she feared, the man.

Deliberately, she concentrated on the object next to the last photograph. The pictures had been a surprise—but not as much as the toys.

Scattered over the shelves of the bookcase was a museum collection of antique...well, there were more serious-minded names for them like clockwork or mechanical, but the plain truth was that they were windup toys! When she'd first seen them, she had almost laughed aloud her astonishment at discovering a whimsy—in Quinn Eisley!—that she would never have believed, much less ever guessed. She sobered a little at the realization that there were far deeper and richer depths in him than she had ever suspected—and that she was coming to know some of them.

Reaching for a blue plush dog, she caught herself and pulled her hand back. "How long have you been collecting them?"

Quinn picked up the dog and put it in her hand, indicating that she should wind the key in the dog's ribs. "Fifteen or twenty years. They always fascinated me as a kid."

Carefully she turned the key, then laughed as the dog clapped its paws, trotted a few paces across the rug, its long blue ears flapping, before stopping to blow a tinny blast on the tiny trumpet mounted in front of its muzzle. The complete goofiness of it charmed her. She laughed up at him in unabashed delight. "Can I try another?"

It was the first time he had heard her laugh for no more reason than simple happiness. Low and a little husky, it would haunt the room, like her scent. "Take your pick," he said, gesturing toward the bookcase.

Minutes later Blue was kneeling on the rug in the middle of a clockwork circus. "I used to collect antique perfume bottles," she murmured absently as a tin pony with a Wild West Indian mounted on its back reared, then spun on its hind legs while its tail wound crazily and the Indian brandished a tomahawk. "John gave me the first one, for my sixteenth birthday."

It had been cut Irish crystal with a silver stopper, and it had melted into a shapeless black lump in the fire. Nelson had told him about it in another attack of that uncharacteristic garrulousness. It was, Quinn thought, as if Nelson were trying to . . . share her with him. She grinned at him as a thirties gangstermobile made its getaway, sparks firing from the machine gun stuck out the rear window. He'd seen wistfulness when she'd mentioned the perfume bottles, but as quickly as it had come, it was gone, as if a second or two were all she would permit herself to feel it.

Blue wound up a fur-covered camel and watched its lifelike pitch and roll toward the man hunkered across from her as the tiny tin driver—complete with red felt fez—jounced on its back. Although he'd put the toys back in working order, he hadn't touched up any nicks and scratches or patched any of the worn plush and fur, and she was glad. The signs of their long lives, rather than restored perfection, added to their charm.

The camel lumbered to a halt, and she gave in to temptation, picking up a toy she'd already played with once. If she had a favorite, it was this one, a rare clockwork music box combination. She wound the two keys in the base, then flipped a lever and the organ grinder began cranking "Pop! Goes the Weasel" out of his hurdy-gurdy while his monkey danced a jig. On "Pop!" the monkey turned a somersault.

As the music wound down, he shifted slightly, nothing more than a subtle flex of muscle, an infinitesimal tightening of the khaki over his thigh, and Blue realized suddenly how foolish she had been to come here. She hadn't thought—no, she wouldn't lie to herself. She *had* thought about the risks of seeing him again, the risks of knowing more about him; tonight, she had just refused to remember them and yielded to the temptation, underestimating the danger. A week ago, when he asked her if she were afraid of him, she'd said no. She knew he would never deliberately hurt her physically, but still she should have heeded his warning that she should be afraid because he could hurt her in other ways. She had lived through the soul-killing pain of loss once already, barely. Chancing any more pain seemed like an insane risk. What she had learned and seen here tonight only made him that much more a real, fully dimensional man—and that much harder to ignore. His head moved a few degrees, letting the light overhead pick out new glints in his hair. Very much harder to ignore.

"These are marvelous," she said, standing up with two of the toys in her hands and a bright smile, "but it is getting late. I should be going home." Turning to put the toys back on the shelf, she felt his gaze on her back like a magnifying glass focusing a ray of the sun, narrowing it until it burned through her.

Frustrated at her sudden withdrawal, Quinn stood up, too. "A car is coming to take you home."

Her head turned sharply toward him as her hand paused halfway toward the shelf. "A car?"

He nodded confirmation. "I have to go back in tonight."

The phone call earlier, Blue thought. Whatever it was, it wasn't an immediate crisis, but enough of one that he had requisitioned a car and driver from Damage Control to save him the time of taking her home. "Another theft?"

He took the toy out of her hand and placed it on the shelf. "Possibly. It hasn't been officially confirmed."

Automatically, Blue began picking up the toys and handing them to him. "Did the bank clerk recognize anyone in the photos John showed her?"

His hand clenched, almost crushing the fragile tin of the blue-and-silver zeppelin he was holding. Had Nelson revealed the purpose of his trip to the Bahamas to her? Something he hadn't revealed to his own men? Quinn wondered sardonically. His ingrained wariness answered. "Roy Durbidge is handling the bank."

She gave him a dry look. "The clerk who opened the Universal Exports account is on vacation, and when John mentioned a trip to the Bahamas, I knew it wasn't to work on his tan. The only reason he would go himself would be because he suspects someone within Damage Control. And it only makes sense that he would take photographs of everyone who's a possibility."

If he'd had any doubts about how well she'd done her job at Justice, they were settled now. Even so, he considered keeping her in as much ignorance as possible, but she was in as deep as he was. He cursed impotently. Damn Nelson. "She didn't recognize anyone."

"You think it's someone inside Damage Control, too," she said quietly as she handed him the last toy.

"It's possible that it could be an outsider, but—" his faint smile was twisted "—I wouldn't bet money on it. The setup of the deal, using Heaney, points to someone familiar with the illegal-arms trade—" his flat tone turned ironic "—one of Damage Control's main areas of interest. Anyone at the briefing last week could have handled it, the only ones in Damage Control who could have, in fact. They all have the field experience, except Ladwig, access to the codes and enough computer proficiency.'' He paused a beat. "Just like I do."

She didn't hesitate even a fraction of a beat. "It wasn't you."

He looked at her, his eyes shuttered. "How do you know?"

"I know," she said simply.

The soul certainty in her answer was an iron fist slamming straight into his chest. Trust was something that he had lived without for so long that he often doubted it even existed. And she had just made him a gift of hers so naturally, so unselfishly. He looked down into her clear blue eyes. And she didn't even realize what she had done.

"The car will be here any minute."

Wondering at the harshness in his voice, Blue followed him back into the living room. "A car really isn't necessary," she said, picking up the gym bag that she'd left by one of the easy chairs. "I could easily have taken a cab."

"It's necessary." He took the gym bag out of her hand and dropped it on the seat of the chair.

Her chin lifted in automatic challenge as she started to ask him what he was doing, but the words jammed in her throat as he slid his hand into her hair, his long fingers grazing her scalp, producing small uncontrollable shivers. His fingers applied an implacable pressure, bringing her to him as his thumb applied more pressure under her jaw to turn her mouth up to his.

Quinn felt her helpless reaction as he watched her eyes widen and darken. He felt a hot surge of anticipation, stronger even than the second time he'd ever had sex, when he'd known what to expect. And it came from just anticipating a kiss. Consciously he slowed his hand, letting the rush build, for both of them.

Blue saw the deliberate calculation in his eyes, and automatically she brought her hands up between them to push against the solid wall of his chest. He was only touching her with one hand; she could break his hold easily, yet the simple strength needed to do it wouldn't seem to come. A stronger shudder caught her off guard, and she closed her eyes against the erotic chill with an unconscious whimper, her hands clenching into useless fists against his chest.

His mouth closed over hers, and a last small remnant of self-preservation tried to resist its persuasive demand.

"Kiss me back, Blue. Open your mouth," he muttered against her closed lips.

A hot pang jabbed through her belly, and she obeyed. His tongue curled in her mouth in a slow, hungry tasting as the kiss became deeper and harder. Her fists opened, and her hands slid up his chest to his shoulders, her fingers kneading the layers of hard muscle with small, restless, hungry motions.

Her blood became a slow fire licking through her as the kiss seemed to go on forever, drawing her in deeper and deeper until she was up on her toes, pressing against him. Her breasts and thighs and belly tightened until they ached, making her strain to get closer still, and she couldn't stop a small satisfied groan when his hand slid down her back to her hips, pulling her into even more intimate contact. His answering growl came from deep in his throat as his big hand spread and began a slow rotation, rubbing their bodies together, rubbing the aches in bone deep.

The hand in her hair dropped to her shoulder and smoothed blatantly over her breast. Her entire body jerked, and she felt him smile a little at her helpless reaction. Searing heat flashed through her, almost making her cry aloud as his thumb stroked over her stiffened nipple. Then his hand cupped her through her shirt, her aching nipple pushing at his warm palm. The back of her throat burned, and her eyes stung. How could she have forgotten what passion felt like? How it felt to need—and be needed—like this?

The stark realization that she had never felt this depth of passion, of need, gave her back a measure of the control she was too close to losing. Pulling her mouth free, she turned her face into the strong curve of his throat. His arms crossed over her back, holding her tightly against him as his hot mouth moved over her face, kissing her temple, her cheek, the corner of her mouth, the curve of her jaw, the shell of her ear.

A small tremor worked its way through her body, and Blue pushed against him. He released her, and she moved back, putting some desperately needed distance between them. Ignoring the chill she felt at the sudden loss of his hard heat, she raised a shaky hand to push her hair away from her face. Her voice was as unsteady as her hand. "It's ... too much."

"It's not enough," he said, his voice a dark rasp. The kiss had lived up to the anticipation; his blood was still pounding. He had never married, never had a "relationship." Sex was casual. The reality of his life dictated that he not follow predictable patterns, so he didn't sleep with any woman on a regular basis and always limited the number of times. The women understood that, and the arrangement had satisfied him—until now. Now he was tempted to forget casualness and a number of women and careful limits. He wanted one woman—Blue Harrell—and he wanted her over and over and over, unlimited, countless times. And sex wouldn't be casual. It would be hot and sweaty and endless, until the bed was wrecked and their bodies were too exhausted and drained to move—until the next time.

In many ways he wished Nelson had never let her cross his path. She was everything he wanted and nothing he needed. He resented her intrusion in his life, resented the temptation of her. He wouldn't give in to the temptation, but he could have her. For a time.

Blue shook her head with a tight helpless laugh as she tried to think of a way to make him understand. Should she tell him that she didn't want more—when she was a mess of aching want? Tell him she didn't need more—when her body was stridently reminding her that a pillow was a less-than-adequate substitute for a hard, warm body? Perhaps she should tell him that she was afraid—when she had been clinging to him, her mouth as hungry as his?

The knock on the front door seemed startlingly loud in the charged silence. When he opened it, the young petty officer on the doorstep came to attention with a sharp salute. "Sir!"

He returned the salute, then reached back for her gym bag and handed it to the driver. "Take Mrs. Harrell home, Montoya, and be sure that you see her inside, to her apartment door."

He stood aside, and as she passed him, Blue looked up. In his eyes she saw the same warning he'd given her when he'd left her apartment after the last devastating kiss: they weren't finished. "Good night," she said quietly.

Chapter 7

"The sale is going to be in Atlantic City."

Quinn sensed the surprise around the table as he took his seat. The location surprised him, too, but the information had come from one of "O'Rourke's" most reliable sources.

"When?"

He answered Nelson's question. "Tomorrow night. All prospective buyers are to be at the Royale Casino at ten-thirty. Maybe the ghost of Ian Fleming will be there, too," he added ironically.

The frowns deepened around the table. "Why Atlantic City, and why so soon?" Glenn Kemper gave voice to everyone's questions.

"Maybe the thief wants to dump them as soon as possible and knows it will be harder to get them out of the country after the armory theft," Tiano offered.

Quinn shook his head. "Compared to a whole car-load of weapons, slipping fifty guns out of the country would be no problem, even now. He could ship them out and sit on them for a month, let rumors circulate, so that when he finally let it be known where and when the sale was, he'd draw more buyers to bid the price up. He's going to lose money, doing it this way," he added dryly.

Roy Durbidge's short bark of laughter came out as a harsh choking sound from his ruined larynx. "Well, maybe you won't have much competition, Quinn."

"He'll have it," Nelson said sourly. "Any weapon that can turn ten men into an army is going to draw plenty of buyers, even on short notice. The dealers know a gold mine when they see it."

Nelson was right, Quinn thought grimly. The Tyrack Assault Weapon was, according to its designer Philip Tyrack, the most perfect hand weapon ever devised. After seeing a demonstration, the United States Navy had agreed and ordered fifty prototypes for field-testing. The TAW-6—the six for its weight, a mere six pounds—was a combination automatic rifle and compact rocket launcher. Essentially two barrels connected by a short crosspiece that served as the butt. What the TAW-6 lacked in looks, it made up for in firepower. Equipped with night and laser scopes, it fired either twenty .9mm rounds per second or a miniature Stinger-type missile. Nelson wasn't exaggerating when he said the weapon could turn ten men into an army. One missile had brought down the helicopter drone used in the demonstration.

NO COST! NO OBLIGATION TO BUY!
NO PURCHASE NECESSARY!

PLAY "LUCKY 7"
AND GET AS MANY AS FIVE FREE GIFTS . .

HOW TO PLAY:

1. With a coin, carefully scratch off the silver box at the right. This makes you eligible to receive two or more free books, and possibly another gift, depending on what is revealed beneath the scratch-off area.

2. Send back this card and you'll receive brand-new Silhouette Intimate Moments® novels. These books have a cover price of $3.39 each, but they are yours to keep absolutely free.

3. There's no catch. You're under no obligation to buy anything. We charge nothing—ZERO—for your first shipment. And you don't have to make any minimum number of purchases—not even one!

4. The fact is thousands of readers enjoy receiving books by mail from the Silhouette Reader Service™ months before they're available in stores. They like the convenience of home delivery and they love our discount prices!

5. We hope that after receiving your free books you'll want to remain a subscriber. But the choice is yours—to continue or cancel, anytime at all! So why not take us up on our invitation, with no risk of any kind. You'll be glad you did!

You'll look like a million dollars when you wear this lovely necklace! Its cobra-link chain is a generous 18″ long, and the multi-faceted Austrian crystal sparkles like a diamond!

**Just scratch off the silver box with a coin.
Then check below to see which gifts you get.**

YES! I have scratched off the silver box. Please send me all the gifts for which I qualify. I understand I am under no obligation to purchase any books, as explained on the back and on the opposite page.

245 CIS AJDR
(U-SIL-IM-05/93)

NAME

ADDRESS   APT

CITY   STATE   ZIP

 WORTH FOUR FREE BOOKS PLUS A FREE CRYSTAL PENDANT NECKLACE

 WORTH THREE FREE BOOKS PLUS A FREE CRYSTAL PENDANT NECKLACE

 WORTH THREE FREE BOOKS

 WORTH TWO FREE BOOKS

THE SILHOUETTE READER SERVICE™:HERE'S HOW IT WORKS

Accepting free books puts you under no obligation to buy anything. You may keep the books and gift and return the shipping statement marked "cancel." If you do not cancel, about a month later we will send you 6 additional novels, and bill you just $2.71 each plus 25¢ delivery and applicable sales tax, if any.* That's the complete price, and—compared to cover prices of $3.39 each—quite a bargain! You may cancel at any time, but if you choose to continue, every month we'll send you 6 more books, which you may either purchase at the discount price . . . or return at our expense and cancel your subscription.

* Terms and prices subject to change without notice. Sales tax applicable in N.Y.

If offer card is missing, write to: Silhouette Reader Service, 3010 Walden Ave., P.O. Box 1867, Buffalo, N.Y. 14240-1867

BUSINESS REPLY MAIL
FIRST CLASS MAIL   PERMIT NO. 717   BUFFALO NY

POSTAGE WILL BE PAID BY ADDRESSEE

SILHOUETTE READER SERVICE
3010 WALDEN AVE
PO BOX 1867
BUFFALO NY 14240-9952

NO POSTAGE
NECESSARY
IF MAILED
IN THE
UNITED STATES

Lightweight, made of virtually indestructible plastic and metal alloys, the TAW-6 was nearly perfect. Its only drawbacks were its scarcity and the uniqueness of the missile it fired. However, with whole munitions factories available to the highest bidder since the breakup of the Soviet Union, one prototype could provide the blueprint for thousands. And with the cash-starved republics now controlling the factories that produced enriched uranium and plutonium, a surplus of unemployed physicists and the relative ease with which the missile could be fitted with a miniature nuclear warhead, the TAW-6 had virtually unlimited lethal possibilities. Terrorists and rebel insurgents from Peru to Azerbaijan would pay anything to get their hands on even one.

"Has there been anything more on how the theft was done?" Ritterbush asked, directing his question to the Damage Control chief.

"No. Neither the Librarian nor Sterba has been able to backtrack the false order, although they're certain they will eventually." Nelson's round Santa Claus face was drawn into most un-Santa-like grimness. Although the weapon had been built under a secrecy that made that surrounding the production of the Stealth Bomber look like an eight-party telephone line, it had been fairly common knowledge around Damage Control. Four of them sitting at the table now—Nelson, Quinn himself, Durbidge and Tiano—had seen the demonstration, and Tiano's division had been given the job of handling the logistics of tranferring the guns to the test site. The weapons had disappeared en route, diverted from their destination once again by a false set of computer-generated orders, and although the theft could have been engineered by someone outside Damage Control, just as the armory theft could have been, it was clear that Nelson suspected that the thief was one of his own.

"So Eisley is going to handle the mission?"

Ritterbush's question managed, as usual, to insinuate suspicion.

"Yes, he is," Nelson said neutrally.

"And Mrs. Harrell will—" Dead cold eyes met his across the table, and Ritterbush wiped even the hint of snide suggestion out of his voice "—provide backup?"

Quinn waited with interest for Nelson's answer. He had some thoughts of his own on the idea.

"It's worked well before. I see no reason to change things now." Nelson glanced toward him. His faded eyes, momentarily out of the direct glare of the overhead fluorescent panels, were a darker blue, and Quinn felt a peculiar sense of recognition.

There was a hesitant knock on the door, and Nelson barked an order to come in. Hal Ladwig entered and, after a nervous push at the bridge of his glasses, handed a piece of paper to him. Scanning the sheet, Nelson swore ripely. "This just came in on the flash," he said, indicating that the message had come in scrambled and coded, and Quinn waited for the latest bad news. "It seems the plant that assembled the missiles for the TAW-6 received a fax two weeks ago, changing the number of missiles they were to ship to the weapons lab for inclusion with the field-test units. Instead of one hundred, they shipped their entire inventory—five hundred and thirty-five missiles. The price just went up, gentlemen.''

Quinn pulled open the deep lower drawer of the desk and rummaged through the row of file folders until he found what he was looking for. As he pushed the drawer shut, the door to the office opened and the man entering froze in the doorway.

"Mind telling me what the hell you're doing going through my desk?"

Straightening up, Quinn laid the object he'd removed from the drawer faceup on the desktop. "It takes a real bastard to use his own daughter the way you've used yours," he said conversationally.

The man in the doorway seemed to shrink as the anger abruptly drained out of him, and, for the first time in the years Quinn had known him, Nelson showed his age. Weariness etched in the slumping line of his shoulders, he turned to shut the door, then crossed the few feet to his desk as Quinn stepped out from behind it. Nelson sat down slowly in the padded chair. "Sit down." When he didn't, Nelson added a word Quinn had never heard him utter in ten years. "Please."

Quinn sat down, his eyes never leaving the face of the other man. "Why?"

Nelson met the flat opaque gray eyes levelly. "It was the only way I could think of to save her."

Quinn's harsh disbelieving laugh contained no humor. "Save her?"

Nelson was silent for a moment, then he began quietly. "The first stage of grief, according to the experts, is shock and denial. Then the person goes through anger, helplessness, maybe guilt and fear, but eventually, after a year or two, occasionally longer, the final stage of acceptance and adjustment comes, with the realization that life goes on. Blue went through the first two stages, but after two years, she still hadn't reached the third. Then one day—" his voice slowed as his eyes shifted, to stare unfocused across the office "—we were walking up Fourteenth Street, going to lunch, when she started to cross an alley. She hadn't looked, so she didn't see the delivery truck coming. I yanked her out of the way. The truck couldn't have missed her by more than a couple of inches. When I started to scold her about being more careful, she looked at me as if she couldn't understand why I was upset with her." Nelson's eyes abruptly focused, shifting back to him, and his voice took on its usual brusqueness. "That's when I realized she probably wasn't going to last long enough to make it to the third stage."

"You mean she was—" His throat seemed to close around the word.

"—suicidal? No." Nelson knew by the relaxation of the tension that had suddenly tightened the younger man's body that he'd guessed correctly. "No, she never deliberately did anything harmful, but, unconsciously, I think she was—" he gestured helplessly "—mourning herself to death. She'd lost her son and husband, and a few months before that she'd lost her parents. It was too much at once. She was going through the motions of living, but in reality she couldn't see any reason to." He paused for a few seconds. "So I gave her one. You."

Underneath Nelson's characteristically unemotional words, he had heard a very uncharacteristic emotion—fear. Nelson loved his daughter and had been desperate to save her, but Quinn still wasn't ready to excuse the method he'd chosen. "So you made her responsible for me. You took advantage of the guilt she felt for not saving her family and deliberately put her in danger."

"Yes." Nelson met his hard gaze unflinchingly. "And I also solved the problem of covering you," he added with a small cynical smile, as if Nelson knew what he was thinking.

"Why haven't you told her you're her father?"

Nelson stared down at the picture on his desk for a long minute before speaking. "I met Denise in Tangiers. I didn't know there had been a child until she contacted me almost three years later. She was dying and wanted me to take her . . . *our* daughter."

"Why didn't you?"

"I was undercover most of the time, traveling. . . ." His hand made a sharp gesture. "Hell, you know the life, Quinn. I didn't want marriage, a family. Sex was—" he shrugged "—casual, temporary. Denise understood that."

Quinn heard a disturbing echo of himself.

"She never would have contacted me if she hadn't been desperate. She had no family, no one to take Blue." Nelson sighed heavily. "Louis and Martine had been trying to have a child for years, so they were only too happy to take Blue and keep her parentage secret.

They got the child they wanted, and she got a good home with people who loved her very much." He stared at the photograph for a moment again, then raised his head. "And I've never told her because in all the ways that matter I'm not her father—Louis was," he said matter-of-factly.

And because you still don't want the responsibility, Quinn added silently. "I won't tell her."

Nelson nodded once, abruptly, then gave him a curious look. "How did you know?"

"A few things she said and how interested you were in telling me all about her," Quinn said dryly. Nelson's short laugh was equally dry. "She has your eyes."

"That's all she inherited from me, thank God. She looks like her mother." Nelson picked up the photograph and handed it across the desk. "Did you remember the resemblance? Is that why you were looking for the picture?"

Quinn studied the photograph. He could see a resemblance, although not a strong one. Blue was definitely prettier. "No, I didn't remember any resemblance, and I'm sure no one else will, either." He saw the fleeting look of relief as he handed the photograph back. Nelson immediately put it back in the drawer. "I was just following a hunch. You put it away about the time Blue started covering me." He watched the man across the desk. "I want her with me this time instead of covering me at a distance."

Instantly Nelson was the chief of Damage Control again. "Why?"

"Because now that I know she's there, I want her where I can see her. I don't want to be distracted, wondering where she is."

Frowning, Nelson considered it. "Maybe it would be better to use someone else."

Quinn expressed his opinion in one explicit word. Then, "If the thief is one of us, we don't know who might be compromised. If he's on-site, orchestrating things, he's going to expect to see her somewhere. If he doesn't, he might get suspicious and call off the sale, and it could be months before he surfaces again. We have the chance to get him now." Quinn pressed his point. He didn't trust Nelson not to agree that Blue shouldn't be involved and then send her as his shadow anyway. He might love her, but that wouldn't stop him from using her—the job came first. Only by keeping Blue with him would Quinn have a chance to keep her safe. It wasn't perfect, but it was the only option he had.

"All right," Nelson said slowly. Something wasn't right, but he couldn't put his finger on it. "I'll notify her about the change in plans."

Quinn stood up. "I'll take care of it. We'll leave in the morning. That will give me time to coordinate with the backup you've borrowed from Naval Intelligence."

Watching the younger man move to the door, Nelson at last realized what was wrong. The obscenity Eisley had used wasn't unusual; it was a common, Anglo-Saxon favorite, in fact. What was unusual was that he had used it at all. Quinn Eisley never cursed. And not because of his genteel Old South upbringing, either, Nelson thought cynically. A man had to feel emotion to curse, and Quinn Eisley was one of the most cold-blooded men he'd ever known. If he was cursing now, it meant he finally felt something, something intensely personal.... "No!" he said, coming to his feet in a rush. "You can't have her."

Quinn matched the hard glare of the older man. "Then you should never have put her in my way," he said softly.

Atlantic City was a beautiful facade hiding a decaying interior. And not hiding it very well, Blue decided, pulling the curtain back farther. The Royale was oriented so that guests had a view of the beach and ocean, but with a turn of the head they could also see that behind the glamorous skin of glittering, glitzy hotels and casinos, the body of the city was decomposing. Rows of abandoned and crumbling houses alternated with grimy patches of liquor stores, peep shows, sleazy bars, pawnshops and flophouses as the city slowly metastasized into a slum. Letting the heavy moiré curtain fall back into place, Blue turned back to the room behind her. So good were the illusionists who had created the Royale that it was easy to overlook the blight only a block away.

The Royale was a step—or several—above the other hotel-casinos along the Boardwalk. Modeled after the gambling palaces in Monaco, the Royale offered lead crystal elegance instead of neon garishness. Black tie was de rigueur after eight, and the minimum table stakes kept out the "riffraff" before. Suites were twice the size of her loft, and much better furnished, she thought wryly, glancing around.

"That dress didn't come with a back?"

She hadn't heard the bedroom door open. Her sleeveless dress was midnight blue velvet, knee-length and cut simply with a high neckline in front and none in back. "You wanted to make sure the thief saw me," she said blandly as she turned around.

"He will," Quinn assured her dryly. He set a cordless phone—identical to those in the suite—on the side table. "Tell me the scrambler code again."

Dutifully Blue recited the nine digits. "The backup team is in place?"

He nodded. "The show-and-tell likely won't be until tomorrow night, but they're ready. Tonight we'll just find out who the salesman is."

She watched as he pulled the automatic pistol from the shoulder holster he'd carried in with the scrambler, ejected the clip, checked it, then pulled the trigger several times to test the action before replacing the clip and reholstering the gun. He checked the spare clip, then slipped on the holster and snapped the webbing straps. As a final check, he drew the gun in one fluid, blurred motion. The entire show had taken little more than a minute and had a routine air about it that suggested he had done it so many times that putting on a gun for him was as automatic as putting on a bra was for her. She had known it was, of course, but actually seeing him do it was a graphic reminder that sent a small nasty chill down her spine. "I don't like this. What I've been doing has worked successfully for months; I see no reason to change now." This was the first time she had voiced any objection to the plan that she would openly accompany Quinn. When he had told her about it, she had kept silent, knowing that compared to his and John's experience, she was an amateur, but her growing uneasiness made it impossible any longer.

He glanced at her as he lifted a black tuxedo jacket from the back of the couch and put it on, and she was distracted in spite of herself. He wore a pleated white shirt with black studs and plain black silk tie under the double-breasted jacket, and the stark contrast of black and white made him even more stomach-tightening. The black jacket, cut so that there was no hint of the large deadly pistol under his left arm, fit his broad shoulders and lean body to perfection, and the black trousers accented his slim hips and long legs. Yet even the elegantly civilized clothes didn't quite hide the lethal toughness of the man underneath.

"You'll still be doing what you were doing before," he said, slipping a slim black wallet inside his jacket. "Keeping your mouth shut and staying out of my way. And out of the line of fire."

Her orders were delivered in his usual remote tone. The first two were no less than she had expected, but the third seemed less an order than an . . . excuse? He sounded too tough, too cynical and, paradoxically, too protective. Perhaps now she knew the real reason for the change in plan. "A noble gesture, but I think you have the roles reversed here," she said lightly. "*I'm* supposed to be protecting *you.*"

Of the frustration, anger, guilt and fear he felt, anger was the easiest to deal with. His mouth thinned to a near sneer. "I don't make noble gestures. I just don't want to have to shoot through you."

She suspected that his entire adult life had been a noble gesture. The true measure of a hero was not his bravery or courage or physical strength, but his willingness to defend good against evil. Quinn had spent his life doing that, although he would, she knew, reject the title. "Then I'll be sure to stay out of the way." Her mouth quirked sardonically. "I wouldn't want to spoil your aim."

He didn't respond, but his eyes took on a sudden gleam that might be amusement—or the urge to throttle her. Turning away, she picked up the small beaded evening bag that matched her dress, only to have it taken out of her hand. As usual, she hadn't heard him move, although she had sensed him at the last second, Blue realized. In silence she watched him empty the small purse of a lipstick, the magnetic keycard that opened the door to the suite and the small plastic gun she hated but knew was a necessity. His expression unreadable, he looked from the gun to her, then replaced everything and handed the purse back to her.

She was reaching for it when she felt the catch on the chain holding her diamond lavaliere let go. "Damn," she muttered, fumbling for both the purse and the necklace.

"Hold still. I'll fix it." She heard his impatient command behind her at the same time she felt his fingers pursuing the sliding chain around her neck. Biting her lip, she closed her eyes as hot sparks chased after his fingers. He caught the ends of the chain and drew them back around her throat, and she bit down harder. Obeying his light touch, she bent her head, baring the nape of her neck so he could fasten the catch. The brush of his fingers against the ultrasensitive skin, the slight tugging on her hair as he held it out of his way with the callused sides of his hands, ignited more, even hotter sparks that burned down through her body to smolder in the pit of her stomach. She suppressed the moan, but she couldn't suppress the long erotic shiver.

Quinn cursed under his breath as his hands jerked, almost snapping the fine gold chain. He had seen the shiver and knew its cause. The same sensual response had sent heat pooling in his groin. "There," he muttered as he finally secured the stubborn catch and let her hair fall back into place. The soft curls immediately snared his fingers, and he pulled his hands free, and another quiver went through her.

With a growled curse, he pulled her around and covered her mouth with his. As his tongue dived deep, he tightened one arm around her back, and she melted against him. Immediately, he swept his hand up over her hip and side and closed it over her breast, feeling a surge of satisfaction as the nipple rose immediately and stabbed through the velvet into his palm. His tongue stroked deep once more, then he pulled his mouth away. "I want you," he said, shifting his hands to her upper arms and holding her away from him, "but sex is all it is. Don't fool yourself into thinking it's anything else or that it will last. There's no rosy future to spin daydreams about. When the mission is over, that's the end of it."

Blue felt each brutally cold word like a fist, but not for all the money in the Royale Casino, she decided on a sudden burst of white-hot anger, would she let him know how they hurt. Yet the anger was directed at herself as much as at him. She had known what John was doing when he'd offered her a job. He was giving her a "mission" to try to draw her out of that gray nothingness she had existed in, and she had said yes because yes took less energy than no and the inevitable argument that would follow. If she had understood then the terrible risk she was taking, she would have found the energy to say no a thousand times and win the argument as well. John had succeeded beyond his fondest hopes, she thought on another, sharper gash of pain, as the full realization of how careless she had been struck her. As her husband and son had once been her "mission," now Quinn was.

As Quinn watched, the dazed look in her eyes became a blank coolness. With a quick movement she pulled out of his grasp, then walked to the door and opened it. Pausing, she looked back at him. "It's ten-thirty," she said in a voice that matched her eyes. Then she added, "And don't worry, Quinn, I'll keep my mouth shut and stay out of your way."

Despite its exclusivity—or perhaps because of it, Blue suspected—the casino was crowded. Guided by the firm hand on her elbow, she walked through the marble-and-gilt lobby and crystal-chandeliered main casino to a door half-concealed in the ivory paneling on the back wall. Quinn opened it, and they stepped into a smaller, even more ornate version of the main casino.

They were approached immediately by a man who, in spite of his perfectly tailored evening clothes, looked like a bouncer—because, she realized quickly, that was exactly what he was. "The stake is ten thousand dollars, sir. Each," he murmured in a discreet rumble as he stopped in front of them, effectively blocking their way.

Wordlessly, Quinn pulled two gold chips out of his pocket and handed them over, along with the bill he'd taken from his wallet.

"Thank you, sir." The bill disappeared into the right-hand pocket of the man's jacket along with the gold chips while he withdrew a handful of silver chips from the left and passed them back to Quinn. There were no more than ten. "Enjoy your evening, sir, ma'am," he said, stepping aside.

His hand back on her elbow, Quinn paused on the first of the marble steps leading down to the floor of the casino as if he were looking over the tables to choose the one where he would loose the silver chips first.

"Smile."

Obeying his murmured command, Blue gave him a smile of vacuous greed as befit a woman whose primary function was as an arm decoration. His eyes narrowed, he studied her for a long minute before finally starting down the steps.

The casino glittered, the trappings of the room only slightly more bedazzling than those of the people who gathered together, then broke apart when the wheel spun to a stop, the dice stopped rolling or the last card was played as if performing an elaborate dance. The scene had an air of unreality about it, as if it were a stage set and the people all actors, with she and Quinn about to make their entrance, stage right.

"I feel as though I've wandered onto the set of a James Bond movie," she muttered, stepping off the last step.

"I know." There was a hint of dry humor in his murmured agreement.

As he strolled them down the center aisle, her glance slid over the chemin de fer table. The only players were a thin sallow man and a nondescript one with his hair slicked back into a short ponytail. The former fidgeted with his cards, while the latter pushed a finger between his eyes as if trying to ease a tension headache as the dealer drew another card from the shoe. Frowning, she looked back. She felt a peculiar sense of recognition, as if one of them were someone she knew but didn't recognize because of the makeup and costume he wore as an extra in the movie.

The crowd shifted, hiding the table from view, and she glanced up at the man beside her, debating whether to tell him what she had—or thought she had—seen. From the direction he was looking and his slight frown, Quinn had seen something, too. He looked down at her suddenly, and she nodded to the question in his eyes.

Shifting his grip on her elbow, he began to head them in a seemingly aimless direction that would, she was certain, take them to the chemin de fer table.

"O'Rourke. Glad you could make it."

Blue didn't miss the fact that, as they turned around, Quinn placed himself between the man and her. Tallish with a soft plumpness, the man looked nothing like Heaney, yet he reminded her of him as his hands twitched nervously at his ill-fitting tuxedo.

"Glad you could make it," the man repeated himself. "I'm—"

"I know who you are, Azziz."

He answered in O'Rourke's thick brogue, momentarily startling her. Azziz, too, seemed to be startled that he was known to the other man, and sweat began to glisten on his round face, despite the efficient air-conditioning.

"Yes ... well, then ... if you and ..." Azziz's watery green eyes shifted to her, but no introduction was forthcoming, and he cleared his throat. "If you and the—the lady would—"

With an abrupt movement, Quinn pulled a handful of silver chips out of his pocket and turned to her. "Amuse yourself for a few minutes," he told her, dropping the chips in her hand.

With her hand closed into a fist around the chips, Blue watched him cross the casino. Taking a meandering course as if she couldn't make up her feeble mind which game to play first, she followed. When he and Azziz joined three other men at an idle blackjack table, she turned to the nearest table and dropped a chip onto the first square she saw. Feigning fascination with the spin of the roulette wheel, she watched from under her lashes as greetings—not friendly— were exchanged. The wheel stopped, another silver chip joined hers, and she pushed them absently to a black square.

"Gentlemen," Azziz said, resisting the urge to run his finger around his tight collar, "I think you know each other."

Quinn looked at the skeletally thin man with the pocked face. "It's been a long time, Geringer."

"Maybe not long enough, O'Rourke," the Dutch arms dealer answered sourly.

"Heard you made an ace haul in Belfast, O'Rourke, although the IRA weren't so lucky." The stocky blond Australian, Nance, eyed him speculatively.

His what-can-I-say gesture drew a laugh from Nance, a nervous titter from Azziz and stone silence from the other two. Shifting slightly, he checked the roulette table thirty feet away. Blue, damn her, was obeying the letter, but not the spirit, of his orders.

"Perhaps we could save the pictures of the wife and kiddies for later," the small dapper man beside Geringer said caustically. Carlos DeSouza did most of his business in North Africa, and Quinn was frankly surprised to see him so far from home. "When do we see the merchandise, Azziz?"

"Tomorrow night." The salesman swallowed noisily at the looks of deep dissatisfaction on his customers' faces. "You will be informed of the time and place."

DeSouza waved his hand around the casino contemptuously. "Then why this charade tonight? If you have nothing to show us, why are we here?"

DeSouza knew the answer as well as he did; the Brazilian was simply amusing himself at the salesman's expense. Azziz was just a puppet, dancing to the thief's pull on his strings. Like Heaney, he normally did business in the thousands, not millions, of dollars. And with the production possibilities, it could be multimillions, Quinn thought grimly. The thief had ordered the meeting tonight to vet the buyers. He would either be contacting Azziz to find out who had shown up or, more likely, he was present and knew already. It would be the thief, not Azziz, who would see to the "informing," ignoring anyone who didn't pass the vetting—or setting a trap for him.

"He wanted to make sure we were serious, right, Azziz?" Nance said dryly, earning a grateful look from the broker. At the roulette table, Blue was getting a few looks from one of Azziz's men. Maybe he had heard about Heaney or maybe he was just smarter, but Azziz hadn't come alone; Quinn had counted at least four men so far, hovering around their boss, trying to look inconspicuous. The man crowded a little too close to her, and she stepped back, her spike heel catching his instep and her elbow his gut. He had to admire how slick she was, giving the move every appearance of an accident, but still, he wished she hadn't done it. He wanted Azziz and his men to think of her as a piece of fluff, to discount her as a threat so they would be less of a threat to her.

"I assume there will be a demonstration?"

"Of course," Azziz assured Geringer. "Tomorrow night." Quinn noted the salesman's furtive glance in his direction and wondered at the reason.

"What about the price?" DeSouza continued to complain. "Even the minimum bid is too high. No hand weapon is worth twenty-five-thousand dollars." Nance and Geringer remained silent, content to let DeSouza start the bargaining process.

"Twenty-five-thousand dollars is stealing them." Azziz seemed unaware of the irony of his words. "Every Soviet republic is having a garage sale, driving prices down. One cannot even make expenses," he whined.

His customers ignored him. Nance looked around the group. "'Til tomorrow night, then, mates."

"It seems you amused yourself pretty well."

Blue gave the three stacks of silver chips in front of her a slightly bemused look. "It would seem so." Sweeping the chips into her purse, she stepped back from the table. "How did it go?" she murmured as his hand resumed its customary place.

Working them toward the chemin de fer table, Quinn told her, then asked a question of his own.

"I never saw them again," she said in an undertone as the table and three unfamiliar players came into view. In a more normal tone, she added, "What now?"

Quinn smiled down at her for the benefit of Azziz's two men, stationed a few yards away. "We'll stay and play for a while, to strengthen our cover," he murmured.

Watching him shake a pair of dice a few minutes later, she allowed herself to relax a little, and the anger she had had to suppress simmered up. It was so much easier to live in the shadows of life—no pain, no feeling. Now she was—damn him!—alive again... enjoying...suffering...wanting....

But maybe she wasn't the only one. After that last bone-charring kiss, his breathing had been ragged and a little too fast. Hectic color had run along his cheekbones, and, just for an instant, his eyes had lost their chronic blankness and she had seen something raw and blisteringly primitive. She had almost crowed in triumph at the proof that he wasn't as unaffected as he wanted her to think. Maybe it was the peculiar sense of unreality that had overtaken her when she had stepped on the floor of the casino weakening her normal caution, but suddenly she was determined to see that look in his eyes again, to pull from him the responses he pulled so effortlessly from her.

She was so careful about touching him that the rub of her thigh against his had to be accidental. Ignoring the small rush of heat, Quinn offered her the dice. "Do you want to make the point?"

With an odd little smile, she reached for the dice. Instead of letting him drop them in her hand, she took them out of his, lightly scraping her nails over his palm and the inside of his wrist in the process. His fingers closed reflexively, trying to stop the electric charge running up his arm. He looked at her sharply, but her attention was on the two white cubes tumbling over the red felt to the accompaniment of the excited murmurs of the small crowd around the table. The dice came to rest, and the croupier added to the pile of chips in front of him. She looked up with a wordless question, and he scooped up the pile. "Let's try the blackjack tables."

Reaching for her elbow, his hand landed on her bare back instead as she seemed to sidestep something on the floor. Giving in to temptation, he left it there, enjoying the feel of her cool, smooth skin as if it were a furtive, forbidden pleasure. It would be so easy to slide his hand down, to— He blanked out the thought, but not before he felt it in the pit of his gut. The firm muscle under the satin skin shifted as she walked, subtly stroking his palm and suddenly his hand felt on fire. Only at the last split second did he stop himself from snatching it away. Instead, he moved it subtly, he hoped naturally. Then, closing his burning fingers into a tight fist, he jammed his hand in his pocket.

She turned, her eyes wide and clear. "How about here?"

It was several seconds before he realized that the question wasn't an extension of his heated subconscious, and that she was asking him if he wanted to stop at this particular blackjack table. "Fine," he said curtly and heard the hoarseness in his voice. He pulled out one of the short-backed, high stools for her and took another for himself. As she sat down after him, her hand brushed his shoulder, her fingertips trailing over his neck and the underside of his jaw. He felt singed. Snapping his head around, he stared at her. After his bluntness back in the suite, was she giving him back a little of his own, making, perhaps, a different point?

She met his narrow stare with another wide, clear-eyed look, and his certainty wavered. "Are you going to play?"

Her voice sounded huskier than usual, or maybe it was his fevered imagination, supplying a double meaning where none was intended. Wordlessly, he shook his head. With a small shrug that drew the dark velvet tight over her high breasts and confirmed his suspicion that she was wearing only skin under it, she turned back to the table. As she reached forward to place her bet, the dress gaped a little, revealing the beginning swell of her breasts, firm and slightly flushed, and his blood began to itch. Her cards were dealt, and she turned up the corner of the hidden one, shifting a little on the stool. Her thigh slid against his from hip to knee, and again he barely controlled his body's instinctive jerk. Carefully he hitched his stool away. She gave him a curious glance, then went back to her cards.

Automatically he scanned the crowded tables around them. There was no sign of the two men who had been at the chemin de fer table earlier, and Azziz had called off his watchdogs.

Her rueful laugh drew him back. "My luck seems to have changed. Why don't you try yours?" One fingernail drew across the back of his hand where it lay on the green felt between them.

He couldn't control the jerk this time, and this time her eyes erased all doubt. Challenge burned in them bright and clear and—damn her—knowing. Her voice turned low and sultry. "What's the matter? You don't want to play?"

His teeth bared in a travesty of a smile as he shoved her remaining chips forward blindly. Dimly he heard the slap of cards as his fingers locked around her wrist. "Stop it!" he ordered in a harsh undertone.

"Why?" More than the word, the angle of her chin and the glitter in her eyes were a dare, and he felt his control slipping away. Slowly she smiled, a smile that said she knew she was making him lose control—and enjoying it. The smile was one straw too many.

With a curse, he shoved back his stool, dragging her off hers.

The dealer determined that the house had won and automatically began gathering up the cards and chips lying on the table. Picking up the pair that had belonged to the couple just leaving, he saw that there was an ace under the grinning jack. "Sir—" he started to call, then saw that they were already too far away. Shrugging, he added the four silver chips to the stack in front of him.

He didn't speak or even look at her as they rode up alone in the glass elevator. In fact, they might have been total strangers, Blue thought, if not for the long steel fingers snapped around her wrist. The moon outside the walls of the glass box was a bloody orange that glowed eerily, adding its illumination to the light strip on the floor, which was deliberately dim so that passengers could enjoy the nighttime view. The faint unearthly luminescence honed the planes of his face and seemed to reflect back from his eyes, giving him an almost satanic look. For the first time, she wondered if perhaps she hadn't succeeded a little too well and unleashed a response far beyond her wildest expectations. The thought was thrillingly satisfying—and a little frightening.

The door slid open with a barely perceptible whisper, and the steel fingers gave her no choice but to follow him down the hall. He paused only as long as it took him to release the jamming device he'd used on the lock; then he shoved the door open, pulled her through it behind him and kicked it shut with a barely controlled violence. Without warning, he wrenched her into his arms, one hand tangling in her hair to jerk her head back. His face was flushed, the skin drawn tight over his cheekbones, and his lips were drawn back in an almost feral snarl. And his eyes . . . As she looked up into eyes that burned with a rapacious hunger, she understood that the fire she had been playing with was going to consume her, too.

"I dream of you." His voice was so guttural that it sounded more like an animal growl than human speech. "I dream of touching you, taking you—fast, slow, hard. Any way. Every way."

His mouth crushed down on hers, and she tasted the anger mixed with his desire. She understood it, relished it, because it matched her own. Yet deep inside her there was a small sob of despair. She had expected . . . not love—never love!—but something . . . something more. . . . His teeth were sharp on her lip; she tasted blood, and then thought was unimportant.

She met his violent demand with her own. As her teeth raked his tongue, she heard a low hungry growl that she only dimly realized was her own. Her hands skimmed up his flanks and back as his hands mirrored hers, sliding over her buttocks and rubbing up her bare back, pressing her closer. Frustrated with cloth instead of skin, she ripped his tie free and was struggling with the studs fastening his shirt when she felt the slide of fabric down her body and a sudden coolness. Her hands clenched in his shirt as his mouth left hers to brand a trail down her throat, over her shoulder and lower. When he took a nipple in his searing mouth, her breath strangled in her throat. Her nails dug through his shirt, and her hips arched, seeking him.

His mouth came back to hers, his tongue hot, driving and insatiable in blatant simulation of the more intimate act. One hand grabbed hers and dragged it down between their bodies to the hard ridge straining against the sober black cloth. It wasn't an invitation to touch him, she understood; it was a demand. Opening her hand under his, she stroked down slowly, then back up, then down again, the friction warming her palm. His hand fell away as hers moved again, her fingers closing, and suddenly she was swinging dizzyingly through the air.

Her feet touched the floor only long enough for him to strip her and the brocade spread and top sheet from the bed. His own clothes went as fast, and then he was on the bed, too, beside her, over her.

Her scent swirled around him like a whirlpool, drawing him in deeper and deeper until he was drowning. Quinn looked down at his hands. He had never wanted a woman until his hands shook. He buried them in her hair, his mouth taking hers, his tongue seeking the sweet sharp taste he couldn't seem to get enough of. Her hands slid over him, hands that had been dipped in fire, dripping flame wherever they touched.

His hands moved over her body, demanding, gripping, pressing. Bruising caresses—and hers were no more gentle. The only light came from a lamp in the other room, but it had been enough for Blue to see the matting of fine soft black hair that covered his chest. She ran her hands through it, and her nails dug into steel muscle while her palms flexed, saturating themselves with the feel of him.

His hands slid up to the round firmness of her breasts. Her skin was like the velvet dress she'd worn, only softer and warmer. His thumbs found the small dark rose nipples and stroked, his fingers kneading while his mouth tested the softness of the skin under her jaw, licked the taste of her from the erratic pulse in her throat, then he closed his teeth around a hard thrusting nipple.

Blue heard her own moan. His hands began moving again, and his mouth, scalding her flesh wherever he tasted her. Her hands began searching, too, seeking the rigid heat she'd only been able to touch through frustrating layers of cloth before. One hard hand slid up the inside of her thigh, finding the unprotected soft warmth between her legs, and her fingers spread convulsively on his belly as the pleasure jolted through her.

Even as she was still gasping, she was fighting, clawing to bring him closer. For a second he hesitated, his body so hard and tense he seemed to be made of stone. Then he drove into her, and Blue cried out at the fullness she hadn't known for so long—so hot, so hard, so *good*. With a little choking sob, she flexed, trying to draw him in deeper.

"That's it—more. Take more," he growled gutturally. "All of me. Take all of me." She opened her eyes to see that every vestige of the remote aloof man had been stripped away. His teeth were bared in a grimace of both exultation and near-agony as he thrust powerfully again. Relaxing her body, she tried to obey and felt him slide deeper. Her neck arching, her head ground into the pillow as she tried to draw air past her closed throat.

His hard palms cupped her bottom, lifting her as he pounded into her, and she felt fused to him. "That's it. You feel so good, Blue, so—" his voice caught as she clenched around him "—good."

Sliding his hands up her arms, Quinn wove his fingers through hers, palms tight. He locked his ankles over hers, fitting thighs, forearms, bellies, pelvises together, matching curves, filling hollows. He rocked his hips, sliding his chest over her breasts, sensitizing every cell as he rubbed his body over hers. Marking her with his scent. Claiming her. In the last lucid part of his brain, he recognized that the act was almost unforgivably primitive, but the savage exhilaration surging through him wiped it away.

His body slid over hers again, and every scorched nerve begged for release. Without warning, the fire storm broke over her, and Blue was taken by the flames, her body consumed and lost in the endless inferno.

Quinn held her shaking, straining body tight against his; then the vicious ecstasy caught him, and he was burning and dying inside her.

Neither of them moved. Finally he raised his head and looked down into her dark, still-stunned eyes. "Again."

Chapter 8

He had never slept with a woman before, not in the literal sense. Not that he was sleeping, but—Quinn glanced down—she was. Even when he was young, he had disliked the feel of another body in the bed. It didn't bother him during sex—which was fortunate, he thought sardonically—but afterward, he couldn't tolerate the crowding, the clinging arms, the crossing of the invisible boundary of solitary space he had established around himself years ago.

She made a small sound, and, without thinking, he eased her closer. Her hand slid over his ribs, and a soft sigh feathered across his chest. She was exhausted; she had fallen asleep almost immediately, their bodies still joined, and when he had moved away from her, she had followed him in her sleep, as if they were still joined.

The first time he drove into her, he had felt a moment of panic because for the first time he knew what it was to have sex with soul and mind involved, not just body. And the part of him that had always been held apart, aloof even in the throes of climax, had been as engulfed as the rest of him in a satisfaction he had never known. The second time, the involvement and satisfaction had been even greater—something he wouldn't have believed. Yet as he lay gasping afterward, too sated to move, every cell in his body steeped in her, he had felt an odd, inexplicable desolation.

She had been in the midst of a lovely dream she couldn't quite remember and, looking up to the empty gray eyes watching her, Blue wished fervently that she could slip back into it. She wasn't ready for reality yet. She needed time, time to understand the volatile emotions that had ignited inside her without warning, time to try to understand the woman she saw in the mirror every morning who had suddenly become a stranger.

She had been married; she had had a healthy sex life. She had thought she'd known all about desire and sensuality and sex. She'd been illiterate.

The near-violence with which they had come together should have frightened her, and it had, but not as much as it had thrilled her. The raw sexuality he had released in her had stunned her—and excited her almost past bearing. Even now, the erotic feel of his hard muscles and the fine silky hair covering his chest and belly and his hot skin against hers lingered. He had imprinted himself carnally on her, inside and out, and the sheer animalism of it ought to have frightened her, too, but it didn't. She had reveled in it, and in his possession. Yet when he had locked their bodies together, she had felt a sudden terror, because it felt as if somehow she were losing some vital part of herself. She had struggled to escape, but then he had started to move, and all desire to escape had been incinerated in the firestorm that had swept her up. But now she understood the terror. She knew what she had been hiding from herself, knew what she had lost—not minutes but days, probably weeks, ago. Her heart. She was in love with him.

His arm reached over her, and his forefinger touched a bluish mark above her right breast. "I always seem to bruise you," he murmured.

She had been wrong. His eyes weren't empty. They were shadowed with regret, and Blue felt a sudden stinging at the back of her own eyes. She rolled away from him, catching the sheet to hold over her breasts as she sat up. He sat up, too, slowly, heedless of the sheet, and his lips were opening to speak when there was an abrupt knocking on the suite door.

He didn't move so much as flow. Without the interference of clothing, she could see even in the dim light the smooth coordination of muscle in his tight hard buttocks and long powerful legs. He pulled on his slacks, zipping them one-handed as he reached for his gun. "Stay here," he ordered. Pushing in the button in the knob to lock the bedroom door, he pulled it shut behind him.

Blue grabbed her clothes off the floor and ran to the door. Cursing the Royale's owners' dedication to quality, which had made them choose solid doors instead of cheaper hollow ones that made eavesdropping easy, she held her breath, listening. All she heard was a wordless murmur of at least two voices. Keeping her ear pressed to the door, she dressed without thought until the moment she started to pull her dress up over her hips. A muscle-melting weakness overtook her as she remembered how the dress had come off and what had followed—his hands...his mouth...his body....

Ruthlessly she shook off the remembered touches, tastes, textures and mental images. Looking around for Quinn's bag, she spotted it on the luggage rack across the room. The metal case had a double locking system, with dual combination and key locks—and the lid was shut, the latches down tight. Anything he had in there that she could use to defend them might as well be a thousand miles away.

Quinn ignored the peephole; it made an assassin's job too easy. "Who is it?" he demanded, his brogue back in place, letting whoever was on the other side hear sleepy annoyance. Even as he spoke, he moved to the side of the door from the one on which it opened, just in case whoever was on the other side was planning a few quick shots. The position was automatic, something he didn't even have to think about.

"Azziz."

"Why?"

"There has been a change in plans."

Quinn thought rapidly. He didn't like changes, but he liked the idea of losing the thief and the weapons even less. He glanced toward the closed bedroom door, willing it to stay closed; then, still standing to the side, just in case Azziz was thinking of rushing him he opened the door.

Azziz looked at the Bren pointed at his heart and felt the sweat start to run down his back. "That isn't necessary," he said in an aggrieved tone.

Quinn glanced at the two men flanking the salesman. "Are *they* necessary?"

Azziz tried ingratiation. "Protecting oneself is one of the unfortunate realities of our business, as I know you understand even better than I." The stony look on O'Rourke's face said he did not understand, and, very reluctantly, Azziz turned to the two men behind him. "Stay here," he said, not liking the look of relief on either of the men's faces.

"I don't like changes, Azziz."

Azziz heard the delicate hint of menace clearly. After shutting the door, O'Rourke had lowered the gun, but it was still in his hand. Absently he pulled out his handkerchief to mop his face as he went into his rehearsed spiel. "My supplier is understandably concerned after what happened in Belfast. He's decided there would be less chance of anything . . . unforeseen happening if the sale were now—tonight—instead."

Moving up the sale didn't give any of the prospective buyers time to set up a double cross, and it cut down on the risk of another hijacking. In the supplier's position, he would have done the same himself, Quinn thought, yet the twitching along his spine that had saved his neck more times than he bothered to remember told him it could be a trap. It wouldn't be the first time, he reminded himself ironically, but this

time a trap wasn't a concern. Blue would alert the
backup team as soon as he left, and the men would be
in place by the time he walked out of the elevator. "If
your supplier is nervous, certainly tonight is as good
as tomorrow night." He added casually as he started
for the bedroom door, "Your supplier was the one in
Belfast, too?"

Stuffing the handkerchief back in his pocket, Azziz
answered with rare honesty. "I don't know. I—haven't
done business with him before."

As he suspected, Azziz, like Heaney, didn't know
who he was doing business with. The bedroom doorknob was in his hand when Azziz spoke again.

"The . . . lady has to come, too."

Starting to say that he had no idea where the "lady"
was, Quinn saw the gunrunner looking at her purse on
the couch and cursed his carelessness. "I just picked
her up in the casino. She has nothing to do with the
deal."

Azziz pulled his handkerchief out again as the Black
Irishman turned his dead-cold eyes on him. "The
supplier would feel more secure if sh—she came."

If he refused, Azziz might well become too suspicious and cut him out of the deal, and if he agreed, he
could be walking Blue straight into a trap. Seeing the
scrambler lying a few tantalizing feet away, he cursed
his carelessness again. He should have made sure Blue
had it before he opened the door; then it would have
been where it could do him some good. Even if it
meant knocking her out and tying her up, he had never
had any intention of letting her anywhere near the sale,
but now it seemed he had no choice. If it was a trap

and he didn't agree to go, Azziz could just have his men storm the room. Given the option, he would rather go, even if it meant Blue had to go, too, because he would have more room to maneuver. "She'll only be a nuisance, but—" he shrugged his indifference "—suit yourself."

She was already dressed and ready to go, he saw as he closed the bedroom door. "You heard?" he asked quietly as he reached for his shirt.

"The last part," Blue answered. "I take it the sale is tonight instead?"

Buckling his shoulder holster, he nodded. "I don't like the feel of it. Stay beside me and—"

"I know. Keep my mouth shut," she said with a ghost of a smile.

"And don't do anything stupid," he added without expression. A raised eyebrow was her only response. Finished with his shoes and socks, he stood up to shrug into his jacket, then reached for the black leather briefcase standing beside the dresser. She started for the door, and he caught up with her just as she was reaching for the doorknob. Grabbing her by the nape of her neck, he jerked her forward and gave her a hard kiss. "Stay *right* beside me," he repeated softly.

The ride down in the elevator passed in silence. The men with Azziz reminded her of the bouncer in the casino, only not as well tailored; the pistol-size lumps under their jackets were obvious. Staring straight ahead, she ignored their leers. After a few seconds she sensed Quinn's head turning, and the men's eyes shifted to the floor.

As they walked out of the casino, the engine of a dark limousine parked at the curb started. With unctuous courtesy Azziz held the rear door open for her as his two men crowded into the front seat with the driver. Quinn sat beside her, and the arms dealer settled on the seat opposite her like a fat toad.

As the limousine pulled smoothly away from the curb, Quinn broke the silence. "Aren't the other buyers joining us?"

The handkerchief came out again. "My...associates are picking them up, so that we won't be too crowded."

That seemed to exhaust the small talk. Blue wished she could roll down a window. The salesman's cloying cologne wasn't quite strong enough to mask the sour smell of his sweat. Quinn sat, seemingly comfortable and unconcerned, his shoulder just touching hers. Despite the mugginess of the night and close atmosphere of the car, a shiver went through her. She felt a subtle shift of muscle beside her, and his hand closed around hers like a warm glove.

The limousine turned off the street, and Blue felt a strong sense of déjà vu. Another dock, another warehouse. The only difference was that the nightwatchman lights here were all working. Except for them, the dock appeared deserted, no other vehicles or people in sight. The car stopped halfway down the row of warehouses, and the men in the front seat immediately threw open their doors and got out. Holding the black case in one hand, Quinn helped her out of the car. Turning around, she was surprised to see the lights of the casino strip scant blocks away, because the drive had seemed longer.

Quinn wasn't surprised when the three "associates" followed them inside the warehouse, shutting the door after themselves. And he wasn't surprised to see the wooden crates in front of the long rows of empty shelving and no sign of Geringer, DeSouza or Nance. He was even less surprised to see two more "associates" materialize from behind the shelving, guns in hand.

"What's this, Azziz? A stickup?" he asked dryly.

"No, O'Rourke, it's a hit, although I will take the money. But first, your gun." Despite his show of bravado, there was a nervous edge to the gunrunner's words.

Slowly he reached for his gun.

"No. Take off your holster," Azziz ordered sharply.

Expressionlessly, Quinn set down the briefcase, then took off his jacket. He had underestimated Azziz. Making him take off the holster made it much harder to use his gun than it would have been if he had simply drawn it out of the holster to hand it over. As soon as the buckle was free, one of the men behind him stepped forward and jerked the straps down his arms and off.

At first Blue thought Azziz's man's rough handling had thrown Quinn off balance and that was why he stepped on her foot. When it happened again, she understood. Carefully she eased off her right heel, then the left. Staying on her toes, she inched the shoes behind her.

Quinn gave the salesman cum hit man a moderately curious look. "Why?"

"My supplier wants to make sure he doesn't end up like the IRA did in Belfast."

He shook his head almost pityingly. "I have friends who won't appreciate this." He saw that Azziz wasn't the only one starting to sweat. He could only hope that the two behind him were, too.

"That's a chance we'll have to take." The nervous edge was sharper. "I'm sorry about the woman," he seemed to feel constrained to add, "but the supplier wasn't sure she wasn't involved, too. And even if she wasn't—" he shrugged apologetically "—she's seen us."

Quinn flicked a glance at "the woman." Her face was tense and paler than it should be, but if she was afraid, she wasn't showing it. And her shoes were off, he noted with approval.

Azziz moved to one of the crates and lifted off the lid to reveal a row of TAW-6s, gleaming dully against their packing. As he lifted one out, Quinn saw that the weapon was already loaded with a missile as well as a clip of bullets. "I did promise you a demonstration," he said with macabre joviality. "But first, the money." The gunrunner held out his free hand for the briefcase Quinn had picked back up after taking off his holster. "We don't want it full of holes."

Whatever Quinn was going to do, Blue decided, he'd better do it within the next five seconds. Every nerve stretched beyond the snapping point, she watched him covertly for some kind of signal, then almost missed it when it came. "The door." It was as if the whisper came out of thin air. Knowing she was within his peripheral vision, she nodded imperceptibly.

"The money, O'Rourke," Azziz repeated impatiently, stepping the last few necessary feet toward him.

"Sod off, Azziz."

The scene unfolded at the speed of an express train in front of Blue. Slamming the briefcase into the gunrunner's soft belly, Quinn knocked him back into the three men behind him, throwing them momentarily off balance. Whirling into a crouch, one bullet from the back went over his head, while the second was deflected by the Kevlar-reinforced case before he discarded it.

The fight was not an elegant ballet, but messy, frightening and extremely explicit. Coming up off the floor in a blur, his leg pistoned out twice in high kicks, and the two men who had been behind them crumpled to the floor, a broken look about them. Spinning even as they were falling, he lashed out again, dropping another man like a stone. At such close quarters, the three remaining men were at a disadvantage in trying to get a clear shot, while Quinn picked them off, making it look almost easy.

As another fell with a high thin cry, his arm dangling at an odd angle, his gun flipped out of his hand. Quinn caught it in a backhanded grab, seemingly without looking. So fast that the shots sounded like one, he fired, and the overhead lights shattered.

Momentarily blind, Blue could hear heavy breathing close by, the rasping sound raking over her raw nerves. After what seemed like several eternities but was probably no more than a few seconds, her eyes adjusted, and she saw a pale pinstripe of light in the pitch blackness. Knowing it had to be the door, she started moving cautiously toward it. The darkness around her was alive with rustlings and scrapings as the others began moving toward the light, too.

She sensed swift movement behind her just as the pinstripe expanded into a full rectangle. For a second a man was silhouetted against the block of light, and then a gunshot almost at her ear deafened her. Her hearing returned in time to hear an explicitly obscene curse just as an unseen hand grabbed her left arm and began dragging her at a dead run away from the door. The sharp crack of automatic weapon fire pursued them.

Silence returned with a startling suddenness, and Quinn stopped so abruptly that she stumbled into him. From the cold metal pressing against her back, she realized they were back in the maze of shelving. She could just see the pinstripe of light, indicating that the door was once again closed.

"Why the hell didn't you run for the door?"

The vise grip on her arm communicated the furious demand his soundless whisper couldn't. She hadn't run because she had been too stunned for the first few seconds to do more than get out of the way, and after that, because she would never even consider saving herself at his expense. Deciding the question was irrelevant, she ignored it. "How many came in the door?" she asked with the same near soundlessness.

"Just the one I missed."

The hand on her arm finally left. The warehouse was so dark that she felt like she could run her fingers through the inky silence. Despite being right beside him, she couldn't see him; even his white shirt was invisible. She felt small movements as if his hands were working at something, but until she heard the tiny snick, she couldn't guess what he was doing. "How many bullets?"

"Three."

And there were seven men. "I don't suppose you have a laser key chain or mini-Uzi disguised as a ballpoint?"

"Damage Control doesn't have a Q branch."

She appreciated the thread of humor. Only a congenital optimist would call their situation anything as good as desperate, yet it amazed her that she wasn't more afraid. She was frightened—she would have been insane not to be—but it was the healthy fear that gave senses crystal clarity and honed reflexes, not the paralyzing kind of a rabbit caught in headlights. The reason she wasn't more afraid was the man beside her. The warmth coming from his body, the brush of it against hers, even the faint scent of his soap, offered a comforting reassurance.

By the sudden stiffening of his body, she knew that he, too, had heard the scrape of a sole against the concrete in the next aisle, no more than a few yards away. His hand brushed over her mouth in silent command, then she felt the brush of his lips against her ear and a soft rush of moist warm air.

"Stay here. I don't want to have to come looking for you."

The utter silence of his movements was eerie. One moment he was beside her, and the next he wasn't.

It took less than a minute for Blue to realize how unsuited she was for waiting. It was a toss-up whether her nerves were going to spontaneously self-destruct or whether she was simply going to go quietly crazy. Never had she felt so useless or so helpless. Straining as she was to hear, the sudden scuffling in the next aisle and quiet snap sounded like cannon shots.

She waited in an agony of suspense for a shout of triumph, but the suffocating silence continued. Then Quinn materialized out of the darkness beside her. Something hard and cold pressed into her hand, and he was gone again.

Her fingers closed around the gun. She had never considered one as more than a sometimes necessary evil, but now there was a certain comfort in its lethal solidity. She went back to listening. Twice more she heard the sounds of a brief struggle and knew he was still stalking through the blackness.

The slight breeze warned her. Her body turned to stone, she waited for another small stirring of the air to tell her how close the man was. Instead it was a sound that slithered down her backbone, the muted brush of clothing against the shelving. In the same aisle, no more than ten feet away. The soft chafing came again, a foot closer. She couldn't see him, but from the steady stealth with which he was moving, she knew he had no idea she was there. The sound came again, two feet closer, and she turned the gun in her hand so that she gripped it by the barrel, the butt exposed. She didn't want to give her position away by firing, she told herself, but knew that was only part of the reason. And she knew that, if she missed, he wouldn't show her any mercy.

Two more feet and she could smell him—stale cigarette smoke and the sharp scent of fear. He was coming down the far side of the aisle, and it was wide enough that he could pass by without touching her. Moving muscle by muscle, she raised her arm over her head. A rasp came from the aisle almost directly across from her, and she swung the gun down like a hammer.

At that instant he sensed her. His head turned, his eyes gleaming whitely in the darkness, and instinctively she adjusted her aim. The butt connected with an impact that numbed her arm to her shoulder, and the man collapsed with a small squeak. Bending swiftly, she pushed at him to roll him out of the way so that Quinn wouldn't trip over him when he returned. *If* was not a word she allowed herself to consider. The fingers of her free hand encountered short bristly hair and a sticky wetness. Dispassionately, she explored the wound at the base of his skull. He wouldn't cause any more trouble tonight, she thought with an uncharacteristically savage satisfaction.

Wiping her hands on her dress, she stood up just as a terrific crash came from the other side of the warehouse. In the second or two that it took her to decide that a section of shelving had toppled over, the warehouse became hell with the lights out. Short jabbing gouts of flame pierced the darkness. Someone, probably Azziz, fired one of the stolen TAW-6s. The bullets intended for the field testing were tracers, she realized, as lines of red fire streaked toward the corner where the crash had come from. Where Quinn was, she knew with sick certainty.

The gunfire in the confined space was deafening, and the stench and smoke from the cordite and the tracers burned her eyes, making it almost impossible to see. Scrubbing at the tears frantically, she searched for him as ricochets and tracers lit up the warehouse like a flashing strobe light, catching men in freeze-frame motion. Then, just for a second, she saw him, running along the top of a row of shelves toward her, a gun in each hand, his face hard and flat and predatory.

No one would ever know if Azziz confused triggers in the dark or fired the missile deliberately. During a momentary lull, there was a hollow pop, then a soft whoosh overhead accompanied by a trailing faint phosphorescence, followed by a blinding flash and an ear-shattering detonation.

By the time Blue pushed herself up from the floor, one side of the warehouse was engulfed in flames. The missile had ripped away most of the wooden wall between the warehouse and the one next to it, igniting whatever was stored in it along with what was left of the wall. For a moment she stared at the ten-foot wall of fire stupidly, then comprehension returned.

"Quinn!" she screamed, leaping up. Her body, still in shock from the concussion, was slow to respond, and she felt as if she were moving through three feet of loose sand as she ran toward the area where she had last seen him. At least there was light now to see, she thought, trying to control her panic. He had been much closer to the missile impact and had probably been stunned by the blast. Resolutely, she ignored the even more likely possibility. "Quinn!" she shouted again, then was seized by a racking, retching cough from the smoke she had inhaled.

Hunkering down, she managed to find clearer air. "Quinn!" She almost sobbed as she heard the rasping croak of her voice; he would never hear it over the howling roar of the fire. Staying in a crouch, she ran on down the aisle, trying to look through the swirling layers of smoke while the heat increased with every passing inch. She had decided that she had missed him somehow and was turning around when the smoke funneled suddenly and she saw a dark shape a yard ahead.

At first she thought he was dead, and an animal scream of denial was rising in her throat when her frantic fingers found a pulse. It was beyond her strength to carry him, so she hooked her hands in his armpits and began dragging him backward. Their progress seemed terrifyingly slow, and she recognized grimly that the race between her and the fire might end in a literal dead heat. The rapidly advancing flames were already flashing the pools of water from a broken water pipe a few feet away to steam, and she could smell their clothing scorching and feel the fine hairs on the backs of her hands crisping.

Stumbling a little, she fell against a shelf. The red-hot metal seared her bare back, and she cried out, but she wasn't consciously aware of it. Every particle of awareness, every muscle cell, was focused on the task of moving his deadweight out of reach of the vicious flames pursuing them.

Finally they reached the end of the aisle, and she stole a glance over her shoulder to make sure of the location of the door. It was closed, and she saw no one else moving in the warehouse. When she looked back, she saw that a spark had landed on his shirt and smoke was already rising from the burning fabric. With a frantic sob she beat out the small flames, then hitched him closer and began moving again. Halfway to the door, she stumbled over a body and staggered to her knees. She tried to stand back up, but, her lungs burning from the smoke, her muscles starving for oxygen, she didn't have the strength. Her breath coming in ragged sobs, she continued on her knees, oblivious of the skin scraping away on the rough concrete.

It didn't register for a few seconds that the air was suddenly cool and fresh, and several more passed before Blue realized why. For several minutes she just lay on the asphalt beside him, gasping the wonderful moist coolness into her scorched lungs. Finally, reviving a little, she dragged Quinn over to the limousine. Dropping on her knees beside him, she saw the dull silver gleam in his right hand, hardly believing what she saw. After being knocked unconscious and dragged God knew how far, he still had a gun in his hand? Prying his fingers loose, she set the gun aside, then swiftly moved her hands over him.

She found a swelling above and a little behind his left ear, but no blood or any other sign of a wound, to her intense relief. As she sat back on her heels, the significance of the limousine abruptly struck her. She and Quinn were the first ones to escape the warehouse, but they might not be the last. They still weren't out of danger. Grabbing a door handle, she pulled herself up on her knees to look in the window, hoping against hope that the keys were in the ignition.

She slumped back down. They weren't. The locked doors would have been no problem, but she had no idea how to hot-wire a car. One part of her training John overlooked, she thought wearily. Absently she rubbed at the dull ache in her forehead. They had to get out of here. She looked down at Quinn, unconsciously brushing the hair off his forehead. His eyes were open and seemed to be focused and tracking, although he showed no other signs of consciousness, but maybe he was coming around. She could move him, if necessary, but they would stand a better chance if he was up and moving on his own two feet. "Quinn," she called softly, "can you hear me?"

Hell, yes, he could hear her! Mentally, Quinn ran through every obscenity he knew. He just couldn't make anything work, not even his eyelids so that he could at least blink to let her know he heard her. It was as if he didn't have any hands or feet. He knew he wasn't paralyzed, because he had felt the heat of the fire, her careful touches on his body, her fingers in his hair. He had felt the exhausted trembling of her body and heard the desperate sobbing of her breath as she dragged him through the warehouse, felt the fire gaining on them. He had tried to shout at her to leave him and save herself, but he hadn't been able to manage even a whisper, anymore than he could now.

She stiffened suddenly, and her head turned toward the warehouse door, as if she were listening to something. Grabbing the gun he remembered taking off one of Azziz's men, she got to her feet and sprinted toward the door. Then he heard what she had, over the sound of the fire and approaching sirens. The intense heat must have warped the metal warehouse door and the frame around it, and someone was kicking at it, trying to get it open.

He watched her take up a position facing the door, and he suddenly knew what she was going to try to do. No! he screamed inside his skull. Get away from the door, Blue, and get the hell out of here! Watching helplessly, he saw the door finally pop open and Azziz come through it in a stumbling rush. As if the action suddenly slowed down to half speed, he saw her left hand chop the gun in Azziz's hand away; then her right hand grabbed the gunrunner's right bicep, and she swung him around, his back to her chest, his body shielding hers as her left arm locked around his neck. The defensive move was textbook perfect and accomplished exactly what it was supposed to. The second man coming through the door saw someone blocking his way and fired instinctively, cutting off Azziz's warning yell. Backing up, she let Azziz's body fall, the gun in her right hand leveled on the second man. Bringing his weapon back to bear on her, the other man kept on coming, and Quinn heard a shot. The man kept moving. His heart frozen, Quinn heard two more shots from the same gun. For an eternity, neither of them moved; then the man began a slow slide to his knees, finally toppling over. Backing away, Blue bumped into the rear fender of the limousine and abruptly sat down.

The useless muscles he'd been cursing suddenly worked. After lurching to his feet, he crossed the short distance to the two men, then returned to Blue, crouching in front of her.

She raised hollow-looking eyes. "He wouldn't stop coming."

"I know," he said quietly. Easing the gun out of her hand, he slipped a hand under her elbow to coax her to her feet. "Come on, sweetheart, we have to get out of here. The fire will reach the missiles any second." Taking her hand, he urged her into a run.

The blast caught them in the back as they jumped from the dock onto a narrow strip of beach. Staggering as she landed, Blue stumbled, and Quinn grabbed her around the waist to steady her. Breathing hard, they both looked back at the hellish inferno; then her eyes met his, stark with the same knowledge that by all odds they should be dead. Suddenly his arm tightened, and their mouths crushed together in a kiss that was long and fierce and thoroughly carnal as they proved to themselves that they were alive.

The shrieking wail announcing the arrival of the first fire engine broke them apart, and they turned again to the nightmarish scene. As the rising fireball blossomed into a roiling orange cloud, Quinn realized with a sudden grim understanding what it meant.

Chapter 9

Two million dollars, the weapons, missiles and ammunition had just been incinerated. An ash analysis of the remains of the warehouse might show traces of the cash, melted bits of the TAW-6s would probably survive and chemical evidence of the missiles would be present, but the atomizing force of the explosion and intensity of the fire guaranteed there would be no way to prove that all the money and weapons had been destroyed. He was well aware that suspicion had fallen on him after the fiasco in Belfast, and now, with no way to account for the money and guns, he was the prime suspect.

It would be assumed that he had staged the fire and explosion to make it look as if the weapons and money had been destroyed. To divert suspicion from himself, instead of disappearing with the two million dollars, he would claim to have survived Azziz's "murder attempt" to shift blame onto him. A year, maybe two years from now, he would retire and quietly drop out of sight. A man could live very well for the rest of his life on two million dollars. That was what the others at Damage Control would believe. He knew, because that was what he would believe if it were another man instead of himself.

At best his career with Damage Control would be over and he would live the rest of his life under constant surveillance as they waited for him to try to disappear and begin spending the money. The two million had been counterfeit, commissioned by a Middle Eastern government in its attempt to destabilize U.S. currency. Virtually undetectable without sophisticated analysis, it would have been accepted at any bank and could have been laundered through the right one with no questions asked. And, as more damning evidence against him, he knew the right banks. The worst scenario—and the more likely one— would be indefinite "detention." Habeas corpus didn't exist for traitors in Damage Control.

Beside him, Blue began to shiver convulsively. She was crashing from the adrenaline high. Quinn wrapped his arm around her to pull her tight against him. She wouldn't escape suspicion, either. If she substantiated his story of Azziz's double cross, they would suspect he had discovered her much sooner and that they had been working together since the armory theft. Even Nelson wouldn't be able to protect her. The circumstantial evidence against both of them was too strong, and he would be forced to take some kind of action against her, too.

Whether Nelson would believe he was guilty, he didn't know. He did know beyond doubt now that the thief was within Damage Control. Azziz had been ordered to kill him because the thief knew his real identity and knew there was no chance of selling the weapons he'd stolen as long as "O'Rourke" was one of his customers. Only he and Nelson had known about the backup team, but the thief might have suspected it or, more likely, have wanted to deal with him without upsetting Geringer, DeSouza and Nance. And, for insurance, he'd ordered Blue's death, as well. For that, Quinn thought dispassionately, he would kill him.

But first he had to flush him out, and he couldn't do that if he were detained or his every move monitored. He and Blue had to die in the fire, too. The explosion and cremating heat of the fire would make determining who had died in the warehouse impossible, and while Nelson and the others might have their suspicions, there would be no way to prove that he and Blue hadn't been in the warehouse when it burned. He could count on the the traitor to cheerlead the theory that they had been.

He knew where they would be safe and untraceable. The difficult part would be getting there—especially when they didn't have a penny between them—and convincing Blue that it was necessary.

The shivering that had racked her had eased, but his hand found chilly, almost icy, skin when he took her arm to turn her toward him. "We have to disappear for a while, Blue," he said and gave her the reasons.

To his surprise, she didn't argue or even ask questions. "All right, Quinn," she agreed tonelessly.

The voices coming closer behind them prevented him from doing more than giving her a sharp glance. An eight-foot chain link fence blocked any exit on the landward side, and the dock was swarming with men trying to save what was left of the warehouses, leaving no option but to go up the beach toward the lights of the casinos and whoever was coming. Pulling her close again, Quinn started walking up the narrow strip of hard sand. His body was still responding sluggishly, as if the messages from his brain to his muscles were taking a long detour.

They had covered a few yards when he stopped again. More than his body was slow, he thought; his head wasn't working any faster. In the reddish glow reflecting off the water, he looked them both over, assessing the damage to their clothes. Streaked with dirt and soot, his shirt was half-open, the studs missing and one sleeve was ripped. His pants didn't look too bad, and her dress looked none the worse for wear, but her shoes were gone and her stockings were in shreds. "We sure don't look like we've spent the evening playing blackjack," he muttered as he ran his hands through her hair to bring some order to it, ignoring the tightening in his lower belly as the silky curls twined around his fingers. Using his shirt cuff, he buffed the worst of the soot off her face, then tackled his own.

"At least you have shoes."

She said it in that same flat monotone.

As he rolled the sleeves of his shirt over his forearms, she tugged off what was left of the thigh-high
stockings she wore. As she pulled the first one over her
knee, it seemed to snag on something, and he noticed
for the first time that both her knees were bloody and
raw-looking. How...?

When she had seemed to stumble over something
and finished dragging him out of the warehouse on her
knees, that was how, he thought grimly. The stocking
was stuck to the drying scabs. She jerked it free,
showing no sign that she felt any pain, although he
knew pulling half-dried scabs off raw skin hurt like
hell. He liked it even less when she didn't show any
sign of pain removing the second one, either.

The voices were close enough now for him to distinguish words. Whoever it was, he wanted to meet
them farther up the beach, where it was darker.
Bending quickly, he pulled up his pant leg and tucked
into his sock the .38 he had taken from her. Then he
straightened up and reached for her arm saying softly,
"Let's go."

Because of the way sound traveled over water, he
had identified the speakers as two men and two
women by their voices long before they were close
enough to distinguish by sight. From their conversation, he guessed that they had been out on the Boardwalk, seen the fire and decided to come down the
beach to investigate. The idea had clearly lost its appeal for the women and one of the men, and they'd
been trying to talk the second man into turning back
with, unfortunately, no success. Automatically he
braced as the four stopped a few yards away.

"Boy! You look like you were a little too close when it blew."

"Yeah." Quinn recognized the voice of the man who didn't want to turn back. He continued walking, intending to go around them. Past the reflected glow of the fire, the beach was lit only by faint starshine, but it was enough for the four to have had a better look at them than he wanted.

"My God, you might have been killed!" one of the women said, looking at Blue.

"Yes," she said with an odd half smile that sent a chill down his spine.

"See, Jack, what happened to them?" The second woman spoke. "Come on, honey, let's go back."

"Yeah, Jack, come on. We're going to miss the last bus," the other man added.

With a good-natured shrug, the man finally gave in. "Okay, let's go back."

As Quinn and Blue drew even with them, the two couples turned around, and Quinn felt the man named Jack staring at him. "Say, didn't you come down on the hotel bus with us?" he asked amiably.

Quinn slowed their pace to let the man catch up. "The bus from the . . . ?"

He paused, an old trick, and the man filled in the name of the hotel right on cue. "Penta."

A number of New York hotels offered bus trips to the Atlantic City casinos as part of their weekend packages. He and Blue needed transportation, and "Jack" had just unwittingly provided it, with an extra added bonus. The Penta was across the street from

Penn Station. "Yeah, we came down on that one," he said.

The bus was boarding when they reached the parking lot. Watching several people board, Quinn saw that they didn't give their names to the driver or show any kind of ticket. It was almost too easy, he thought, as he guided Blue to the end of the short line. He glanced down at her worriedly. She was ominously silent, although she was following him willingly enough. As if she sensed his gaze, she looked up, and he felt the cold on his backbone again. The hollow look in her eyes was more pronounced, as if the mind behind them were slowly withdrawing. Tightening his arm around her shoulder, he whispered into her hair, "You've had a hell of a night, sweetheart, and it isn't over yet. Just hang on."

That was the second time tonight he had called her sweetheart. Blue glanced around her. She knew the people in front of her were close enough to touch, yet it seemed as if she were viewing them from a great distance. Everyone seemed far away, except Quinn. He was the only one who was close, the only one who seemed real. Her gaze drifted over him. He seemed immune to weariness while she was tired . . . so tired.

Aside from several wrinkled noses from the acrid smell of smoke on them, they attracted no attention. Quinn chose two empty seats surrounded by several full rows to avoid the chatty Jack, and put Blue in the window seat. She seemed to fall asleep even before the bus pulled out of the parking lot. Easing his arm around her, he guided her head to his shoulder and closed his own eyes. Sleeping was a risk, but he probably wouldn't have another opportunity for twenty-four hours. Setting his internal alarm clock for two hours, he gave himself up to the luxury of sleep.

He woke as the bus passed Times Square. Glancing down, he saw that Blue's eyes were wide and unblinking, as if she was staring at something only she could see. He was beginning to suspect what, and the suspicion didn't reassure him. Touching her bare arm, he felt the same iciness he had felt on the beach several hours before. Her dress didn't provide much warmth, but the cold, he knew, wasn't external. It was deep inside her, and, if his suspicions were correct, getting worse. And there wasn't a damned thing he could do about it.

The bus pulled up in front of the hotel a few minutes later, and he waited until it was almost empty before standing up. His natural sense of caution made him precede her down the aisle and down the steps of the bus, and she followed without prompting. Taking her hand when they got outside, he headed for the street and the railroad station on the other side. Even at four in the morning, they had to wait for a break in the steady flow of traffic. A momentary lull finally came when the lights changed half a block away, and, her hand still tight in his, Quinn hurried her across the street. Halfway across, there was a hard jerk on his hand when she seemed to stumble, and, looking around, he saw that she was limping. Guilt jabbed him hard as he realized that he had forgotten she was barefoot. Scooping her up swiftly in his arms, he sprinted for the curb, reaching it just ahead of the next wave of cars.

Once inside Penn Station, he set her down again. She swayed as her feet touched the marble floor, and he was reaching for her again when she seemed to steady herself. Keeping a hand ready on her waist, he steered her across the lobby to a schedule board. He scanned the listings until he found the one for the next Metroliner to Washington, D.C., then looked around until he saw a sign with the right track number.

Like the street outside, the station was far from empty, yet her bare feet and his rough appearance attracted no attention. Thanks to New Yorkers' religious avoidance of looking at each other, he thought humorlessly. Still, unwilling to press the extraordinary luck they'd had so far, he waited for the rush that always follows the final boarding call. The first car was nearly full, but in the next he found what he wanted. Choosing seats near the back of the mostly empty car, close to the bathroom, he again installed Blue in the window seat.

The overhead lights dimmed as soon as the train started to move. Two passengers switched on the individual reading lights over their seats, but the rest took advantage of the chance to sleep. The passing tunnel lights flashed through the windows, but soon the train was out in the open night, and the darkened car assumed an odd coziness. Quinn watched through the window in the door between their car and the one ahead. "Stay awake," he said in a low voice that carried no farther than the woman beside him, although he suspected the warning was unnecessary. He wa certain that if he looked at her, he would see her eyes wide and staring again at nothing he could see.

Twenty minutes passed before he saw the conductor moving through the car ahead of them, checking tickets. When she was five rows from the back, he stood up. In response to the tug on her hand, Blue stood up, too, and followed him as he moved unhurriedly toward the back of the car as if they had decided to change seats. He opened the outer door, using the noise to cover the sound of the bathroom door opening. By the time the door between the cars closed on its own, they were inside the bathroom, the door once again shut.

The cubicle would have been cramped with just him; with both of them, there was hardly room to breathe. Leaving the light off and the door unlocked, Quinn maneuvered them so that the door could open halfway and yet the bathroom would appear unoccupied. In his experience, conductors usually opened a bathroom door only partway when checking for stowaways, and he sent up a silent request that this one wouldn't be the rare exception to the rule.

Her feet between his and his arms wrapped around her to pull her back tight against him, Quinn tried to forget the firm warmth pressed against his groin as he listened for the approaching conductor. The door at the front of the car opened; then there was silence. Blue shifted minutely, and he gritted his teeth against the sudden heat between his thighs while he mentally timed the conductor's progress through the car. He had her about midpoint when the bathroom door was suddenly thrust open. The door swung past midway, and he felt Blue shrinking against him. The light illuminating the exit shone into the cubicle, advancing steadily with the door.

Half a centimeter from his left shoe, the door and the light stopped; then the door swung shut, and a second later he heard the exit door open. As he exhaled slowly, Blue slumped against his arms, and he let them stay crossed over her chest a little longer before finally moving his hands to her shoulders and setting her away from him. After a quick check to see that the conductor had her back to the door and that nobody else was interested, Quinn pushed the bathroom door open.

Three hours later, the Metroliner pulled into Union Station in downtown Washington. Quinn hadn't allowed himself to sleep; whether Blue had, he didn't know. Her eyes had closed soon after they had gone back to their seats, and when he had eased her seat back to a more comfortable position, she hadn't stirred, but he had the feeling that she hadn't slept any more than he had.

They were in position, ready to get off as soon as the outside door opened. The next ten minutes were the most dangerous, Quinn knew. They only had a few blocks to cover, and the morning rush was just starting, but, unlike New York, their worse-for-wear appearance was going to be noticed. And it could very well be noticed by someone who recognized him, since their destination was only two blocks from Damage Control headquarters. He had thought about finding someplace to lie low until dark, but had decided the risk was outweighed by the need to get them under permanent cover as fast as possible.

Thanks to a convenient alley and the luck that still seemed to be with them, they arrived at the parking garage without incident. Quinn couldn't be certain he hadn't been seen, but in a few minutes the problem would be moot. They might know he was alive, but they would have no idea where to find him. Unlike most, the parking garage was accessible twenty-four hours a day, three hundred sixty-five days a year, one of the reasons he had chosen it. Since space was rented by the month only, there was no need for an attendant who might notice comings and goings, another reason he had picked it. Access was gained through a code punched into either the keypad by the street door or the one at the entrance ramp, with each client's code individualized, like an automatic teller machine's pin number.

A few minutes after punching in his code, Quinn started the engine of an older Jeep Cherokee with the spare key he kept hidden under the front end. Letting the car idle for a few minutes to warm up, he watched the woman sharing the front seat with him. Utterly still, she never looked at him, and he was almost relieved at that. The last time she had, he had seen nothing in her eyes, the hollowness complete.

Blue guessed they had been driving for several hours. She wasn't sure, and it didn't matter. She vaguely remembered smaller towns and trees and hills, but it was almost as if the eyes seeing the towns and trees and hills belonged to someone else. She stared out the misted side window. Heat was swirling around her feet, and a while ago Quinn had tucked a blanket he'd gotten from somewhere, maybe out of the back of the car, around her. But she was still cold. Which was funny, actually. She laughed softly to herself. The fire had been so hot, yet she was so cold.

It was hard to see out of the window because of the mist. Or was it rain? It wasn't important. The color-less gray suited her. Through the gray, she caught a glimpse of something darker. He seemed to be slow-ing down, and she could see better. It was a house, a deserted house, decomposing, the empty sockets of its broken windows staring back at her sightlessly.

How had he known to bring her here? Oh, well, what did it matter? It was perfect.

Chapter 10

Quinn brought the ax down onto the massive knot, and it split in half. He was beginning to understand what had driven Nelson to such desperation that he had risked his daughter's life in order to save it. He was about ready to try something equally desperate, and after only a week, not two years. She was like a small animal that had been hit by a car and crawled off into the bushes to die, only it was her spirit, not her body, that had received the mortal wound.

He knew what had caused it. The warehouse fire had been a horrific reminder of the fire that had taken her family, and she had slipped back into the hideous memories of that time. There had been one important difference this time: she had saved the person she had gone after—him. But that didn't seem to be enough. Complicating the situation was the fact that to all intents and purposes she had lost every physical possession. She hadn't, in actuality, but by bringing her here where there was nothing familiar, nothing of her own—no clothes, no furniture, none of her tools—it must have seemed that way. And then there was the new horror of having to deal with the fact of having killed a man. Never mind that the man had been trying to kill her; he knew her well enough to know that she would have had a hard time accepting the necessity of it under the best of circumstances, much less now, under the worst.

He jerked the bit of the ax out of the chopping block where it had buried itself and set up another piece of wood, the stump of a hundred-year-old white oak felled by lightning, then swung the ax high over his head. For the first two days she had done almost nothing but sleep, and he had allowed himself the vain hope that she had only been exhausted, and that when she finally woke up, she would be back to normal. The ax head caught the sunlight as it arced down, sending a brilliant flash across the meadow behind the old house just before it slashed the stump in two. Instead she had woken up with a maddening, almost catatonic passivity that left him feeling frustrated, angry...and helpless, because there didn't seem to be any way to break through it. She cooked, cleaned, had even pulled up all the weeds around the front porch and tied up some vines she'd found underneath. Physically, she functioned, but emotionally—she was beyond his reach.

Standing up one of the stump halves, he began chopping off precise chunks of kindling. As important as it was to discover the identity of the traitor within Damage Control, Blue was more important. He couldn't help but feel responsible for what had happened, and until he found a way to reach her, the matter of the traitor was on hold. All he wanted was a reaction, any reaction, even anger. He had tried to deliberately provoke her. She could snarl, claw and scratch at him; at least he would know there was something in her, fighting to survive, would see some sign that she was healing. He'd gone so far as to let her struggle with the old gas stove that had come with the place, not telling her the trick to keeping the burners lit. He had certainly been "provoked" until he'd discovered it. But...nothing. Two hours after he had first seen her try to light it, she was still trying to puzzle out the problem with the same robotic lack of emotion. Sometime in the third hour she had found the almost invisible valves that controlled the airflow to the burners.

He had considered using sex to reach her. Her overwhelming response the first time, emotional as well as physical, tempted him to try it, but the knowledge that if she didn't respond it would be no better than rape stopped him. That was a risk he wouldn't take.

Gathering up the kindling, he carried it over to add it to the chest-high stack beside the back door. Brushing the wood chips off his jeans and black T-shirt, he frowned absently at the house. He had never consciously thought of it as a bolt hole, and even though that was what it had become, he knew he hadn't bought it for that reason. He had discovered it by accident one summer. The house had started out as a one-room rock cabin built around the turn of the century. Several additions had been scabbed on with a variety of exterior finishes, all of them involving wood in some form. The wood had worn to the color of silver, the steep tin roof was rusted and, after twenty years of abandonment, the three metal chimneys had been more horizontal than vertical the first time he had seen it. Now the wood was still silver, the roof was still rusted, although it no longer leaked, but the chimneys were fully upright.

What had drawn him was the setting, not the house. Near the Maryland-West Virginia border, there was a clean, soothing beauty and uncompromising honesty in the green hills that rolled away to the horizon and the harsh gray limestone that was an antidote to the ugliness and dirt, the danger and deceit, inherent in his job. It was a job and a battle he was committed to totally, but sometimes he needed to be reminded that there was a brighter, cleaner, safer world than the one he lived in, the world that the job and the constant battle preserved.

To maintain the division between the two worlds— and because of the realities of the one he lived in—the property wasn't registered in his own name. Neither was the Jeep he used to get to it, or the parking space where the Jeep spent most of its time. He had never come without the long-range beeper that kept him within reach if he were needed in an emergency, but no one knew where the signal went. His neighbors were hill people and a small community of Amish who had little curiosity about him and thought nothing of his irregular visits. Until Blue, no one from his other world had known he owned it, not even Dekker, the only man he had ever trusted enough to call friend. The secret had been for Dekker's protection, not his own. A wise decision, it appeared now, he thought with a sudden grim fury as he opened the back screen door.

"Lunch is ready." Just like everything else she'd said for the past week, the announcement was made with unsmiling politeness. A smile was too much to hope for, he knew, but he would be happy with anything different, even crossing her eyes and sticking her tongue out at him.

A pot of stew, a covered plate of fresh biscuits and a bowl of canned peaches sat on the table. He knew before he picked up his fork that the stew would be delicious and the biscuits light and flaky. Blue was a startlingly good cook, even with the limited supplies she had to work with, although why he was startled to find it out, he didn't know. Perhaps because the contents of her refrigerator and cupboards had leaned more toward basic nutrition than real meals. He hadn't gone into the nearest town yet for more supplies, because she had shown no inclination to go whenever he broached the subject, and an unnamed uneasiness had kept him from leaving her alone.

"What would you like to drink?" she asked as he washed his hands at the old enamel sink.

"I'll get us something from the pantry." The "pantry" was a glorified closet off the kitchen. He came back with two brown bottles. Popping off the tops, he set one at each place, then sat down.

She picked up her bottle, but instead of mechanically taking a drink the way she had been doing everything for the past week, she looked at the label on the bottle.

She didn't cross her eyes or stick out her tongue, but the expression on her face was almost as good: extreme disgust, with a healthy measure of loathing. "This stuff tastes the way I've always suspected mold tastes," she stated, setting the bottle back on the table with a solid thump.

Intuitively, he knew the best reaction would be no reaction. "You don't like stout."

She gave him a milder version of the look she'd given the bottle of dark, malty-tasting ale, adding a shudder. "No."

Was it going to be that easy? He just had to find something she hated the taste of? No, he saw that the hollowness was still in her eyes. It wasn't going to be that easy, but it was a definite breakthrough. "Stout is an acquired taste," he said mildly. Pushing his chair back from the table, he stood up. "I'll get you something else. What do you want?"

"Anything," she said as he opened the door of the small refrigerator. "Except that can of vegetable juice with the black stuff all over the top," she amended hastily. "It looks like it's been in there at least three years."

"Closer to four. How about a Coke?"

"Fine."

Closing the refrigerator door, he made a decision. "We have to go into town after lunch."

"Why?"

Most of the hard-won expression vanished, making Quinn wonder if he'd pushed her too soon. "Because we need more food, and you need clothes."

"I have clothes."

"Yeah, mine. And I want them back."

It took a while, but a tiny smile finally hovered at the corners of her mouth. "Okay. Yours leave something to be desired in the fit, anyway."

"Beggars can't be choosers," he pointed out as he picked up his fork.

She was mostly silent on the ride into town, but it wasn't the dead, heavy silence he had come to despise. She broke it with occasional comments, and she watched the passing scenery instead of staring blindly ahead at fires that existed only in her memory. Deliberately he chose the long way, taking her through the small Amish settlement first.

Blue watched black pants and jackets flapping like giant blackbirds on the clothesline beside a neat, white farmhouse. Behind it, green farmland rolled to the feet of the timeworn mountains in the hazy distance. A horse-drawn buggy had passed them a few minutes before, going in the opposite direction, and Quinn had returned both the slow, dignified nod of the farmer driving the buggy, as well as the shy grins of the two little boys, who were miniature versions of their father, minus the beard. They passed the schoolhouse, empty for the summer, but out in the yard, their black shoes and stockings discarded, a group of young girls, probably past the age of school themselves, since formal education for most Amish children ended with the eighth grade, were celebrating a respite from their chores with a game of volleyball. Such was the sense of time held back in the little valley that it was the net and ball and not the girls' white caps, plain old-fashioned dresses and long black aprons that looked out of sync with the rest of the world. In the little valley, clothes and buggies and farm equipment from an earlier time were commonplace; the Amish had succeeded in preserving what would be anachronisms in the outside world. Here, the illusion was strong that the outside world didn't even exist. Here, it seemed, everything was cleaner, simpler, safer, and nothing bad ever happened. Even though she knew it was largely an illusion, she felt a painful envy.

When Quinn pulled up in front of a large frame building that was slowly succumbing to age, she knew she had found another anachronism, a true country store. Henderson's, according to the faded sign. One red gas pump older than she was stood a few feet from the wide steps leading up to the porch. It had gone from regular to unleaded, she noted as she passed by. The two men in worn overalls and small-checked short-sleeved shirts who had been sitting on the steps talking when they drove up, stood up politely as she got out of the Jeep, then lifted their straw hats as she passed them.

"Ma'am."

She acknowledged their grave courtesy with a smile that lingered over the drying strings of green beans hanging from the porch roof and the bright red geraniums and wild ferns potted in rusted tin cans. These, too, she realized, were tough-fibered people who wasted nothing.

The interior was a little dim and surprisingly cool, despite the humid heat. The shelves and display cases held everything she expected: galvanized pails, canned goods, a rubber raft anchored to the high ceiling, bolts of small-checked cotton, gas lanterns strung along a rafter, penny candy that now cost a nickel, pickles in a big glass jar on the counter by the old-fashioned brass cash register, and much more.

The older, spare man—Mr. Henderson, she assumed—behind the counter looked up from a catalog as they walked in. "Well, I was wonderin' if we'd see you this summer, Mr. McBride. You remember that engine crank you wanted? A fella came by a coupl'a months ago, sellin' old car parts and stuff, and I picked one up for you."

Cold reality intruded with a rude abruptness. Here his name was McBride. Several things that she'd just begun wondering about, like why he was paying to keep the Jeep in a parking garage when there was plenty of room for it at his house, made more sense now.

"I don't have much in the way of clothes, ma'am." Blue realized the storekeeper was talking to her, and that Quinn must have explained the problem with her wardrobe—namely that she didn't have one. "I've got jeans that'll fit you, one of the boys' sizes, probably, and work shirts and T-shirts and—" he lowered his voice "—underthings—nothing fancy."

She didn't laugh at Mr. Henderson's modesty or his concern for hers—yet another anachronism. She appreciated it. Perhaps the sense of disconnection she'd felt for the past week had begun dissolving, in part, because of the anachronisms she had encountered today. They were reconnections—to an earlier less complicated time, perhaps, but reconnections just the same. They would make those that still needed to be made, to this day and time, easier. "What about shoes?" she asked, holding up one foot to show him the old leather sandal that Quinn had cut down for her.

Not many minutes later she had a stack of new clothes, mostly jeans and work shirts. All of it, except for the plain white underwear, was for boys, but not having to roll up sleeves and pant legs five times was such a luxury that she didn't mind. She finished tying the laces on a pair of white sneakers and stood up. "I feel like I did when I was a little girl. I always wanted to wear my new shoes home from the store," she said with a soft laugh.

Across the store, Quinn paused with a box of crackers in his hand. Two smiles and now a laugh. He added the crackers to the other groceries in the box on the counter. The cautious hope he'd begun entertaining at lunch grew a little stronger. "Maybe you could wear your new shoes over here and help with the groceries," he suggested.

She didn't smile as she walked over, but her eyes had lost a little more of that scary hollowness. Efficiently, she loaded cans and boxes and packages into the carton on the counter, then picked it up and started toward the table of produce. Taking the box out of her hands, he followed her to the table.

"Most of that is locally grown, ma'am," Henderson volunteered.

She nodded to indicate that she had heard and began adding more items to the box.

"Cauliflower," Quinn muttered under his breath.

"Is good for you," she said firmly, putting a half-dozen nonlocal oranges in the box.

"So are brussels sprouts," he said as a test.

She favored them with a look similar to one she'd given the bottle of stout. "Apples are better." She added a few to the box, and he added a few more.

"Anything else?" she asked, looking up with a third, small smile.

"No," he said, looking down at her. "That's enough, for today."

Blue watched two sunbaked boys swing out on an old tire and cannonball down into the pond below. The music of their laughter floated through the open windows of the Jeep, full of confidence that summer would last forever. The boys passed from view, and she turned to the man beside her. "It occurs to me to wonder where you got the money. Neither of us had a penny when we left Atlantic City." It wasn't until he had pulled a roll of bills out of his pocket at the store that she realized she hadn't considered how they were going to pay for the food and clothes. Since he hadn't been anywhere without her since they'd left Atlantic City, she had to wonder how he had managed to acquire the cash.

The suggestion of a grin played around his mouth. "I had it rat-holed at the cabin."

"You were expecting something like this?" Blue asked quietly.

Even the suggestion of a grin disappeared as his mouth hardened. "No, I wasn't expecting anything like this. I don't own the house or this—" he tapped the Jeep's steering wheel "—in my own name, so using a credit card or a check isn't practical when I'm up here or driving the Jeep. I always carry cash, and I've gotten in the habit of stashing most of whatever I have left when I'm ready to go home, to make sure I don't run short sometime."

"How much do you have?" Neither of them could access their banks accounts when they were supposed to be dead, and once it had occurred to her to worry about money, she'd been making up for lost time.

The grin was back. "Enough to keep you in cauliflower for about six months."

"And no one else knows about the cabin or the Jeep?"

He glanced at her. "You do."

Blue fully appreciated the value of the gift he had given her: his trust. "Who is McBride?" she asked after a minute.

He answered immediately, further increasing the value of his gift. "It's a name I used a few years ago with something that involved the Dekkers. When I needed a name on the deed, I used it again. It's common enough that no one would connect it to me."

Blue sat on the bottom step of the porch, watching night seep into the valley below. The last rays of the primrose-colored sunset caught in the blue-and-white glass insulators on the power line, setting them glowing like a necklace of sapphires and diamonds strung across the valley. Down at the bottom, it was already dark, the lighted windows of the lone house brightening the soft gloom.

A faint breeze brushed her cheek as the first of the hummingbird moths came to sip at the moonflowers twining up the strings she tied two weeks ago. The sweet scent of the opening flowers drifted around her as the light faded, and the large, white blossoms took on a faint luminescence. Two more moths arrived, the soft whir of their wings blending with the two-note song of a cricket and the low whistle of a night bird.

She touched one of the paper-thin flowers. It would only last this one evening, but another would replace it tomorrow night. When she had found the vines under the weeds, they had been pale and spindly. They had managed to reseed themselves year after year, but they hadn't thrived. Since she had pulled away the suffocating weeds and strung the strings, the rambling vines had grown sturdier and taller, their big heart-shaped leaves turning a rich green.

She closed her eyes to concentrate on the scent. Two weeks ago, it had been as if somebody had suddenly pulled the weeds away from *her*. The day they had gone to the store had been some kind of turning point for her. And not just because she finally got some clothes that fit, Blue thought with a smile. Like the moonflowers, she had started to come back. She hadn't come as far as the flowers yet, but she was getting there.

A board creaked behind her, then she felt Quinn settle on the step behind her. His long legs bracketed hers as he pulled her back against his chest. She kept her eyes closed, the better to concentrate now on his fingers slowly kneading across her shoulders.

"What are you doing, sitting out here in the dark?"

The bones in her shoulders and neck melted one by one. "Watching the flowers grow." During the past three weeks he had touched her frequently. There was nothing sexual in the touching, no pressure to respond. It was as if he were just trying to reassure her of the presence of another human being, to tell her that she wasn't alone. There was only one bed in the cabin, and they shared it every night. There, too, there had been no pressure. They both slept clothed, and she tried, out of fairness to him, to stay well over on her side of the bed, but often she woke up in the dark to find they were both in the middle, and she felt him hard against her. There was a kind of reassurance in that, too.

She wanted to respond, but she knew she wasn't quite ready yet. She didn't want to come to him less than whole. His tender, unselfish care of her demanded no less.

Quinn felt the liquefaction of the bones under his hands and cursed silently. The past three weeks should have taught him every nuance of frustration, yet each day seemed to introduce a new one. Sleeping in the same bed with her and not touching her was a torture no sane man would subject himself to for even one night, much less twenty-one of them—so far. Yet he wouldn't have given up even one of them. He knew she tried to stay on her side of the bed to make it easier on him, but once she was asleep, she moved instinctively into his arms. He lay there, so hard he ached, yet he didn't let her go. The feel of her in his arms satisfied a need that wasn't sexual yet was just as strong.

He was well aware that he might never know again that unique, total sexual satisfaction of mind and soul and body that he had found with her. The hollowness in her eyes might be fading as she returned to life, but he had no guarantee that she would ever turn to him again with desire. That one, too-brief time might be all he would ever have of her. His hands tightened involuntarily on her shoulders for a moment, then he pushed her away gently and stood up. "You can have the bathroom first."

Blue followed the sound of mechanical sputtering, coughing and choking coming from the barn. As she reached the door, there was a loud firecracker bang, and a small cloud of blue smoke drifted past her. Cautiously, she peered around the jamb.

Instead of four-legged occupants, the barn now housed four-wheeled ones, the Cherokee off to one side and a Model T in the middle, spotlighted by the sunlight flooding in the main door and down from the open hay doors under the eaves. She and Quinn had spent the past three weeks on blessedly mundane tasks—patching up the small barn, doing minor repairs on the house and building a new well house to replace the one that had collapsed over the winter. In odd moments Quinn tinkered with the antique car he had rescued from the automobile graveyard behind a farmer's house, and from the looks of it, its resurrection was nearly complete. Using a wrench, he adjusted something under the accordioned hood, then started turning the crank sticking out of the front of the car.

"You've finally found the ultimate windup toy, Quinn."

He had never heard her giggle, Quinn realized. Straightening up, he gave her a perturbed look, which provoked, as he'd hoped, another of the marvelously silly sounds.

Wiping his hands on a rag, he started toward her. Along with the clothes he'd left at the house over the years, he'd forgotten a shaving kit once, too, but some mornings, like this one, he didn't bother using it. With a day's growth of beard, the dark T-shirt and old jeans and sneakers, he had a lazy vagrant look that did nothing, Blue thought, to lessen his attractiveness.

"What are you going to do this morning?" Quinn asked watching his fingers tuck a curl behind her ear.

She smiled up at him. "I thought I'd see if the rain last night washed out anything new in the meadow." His eyes had changed during the past three weeks. The cold, empty winter gray had warmed with the kind and gentle care he had given to her, although kindness and gentleness, she knew, were not traits anyone would ever have attributed to Quinn Eisley.

One aspect of his personality remained unchanged, she thought wryly, as he spoke again. He was as arrogant as ever.

His long fingers tucked a curl behind her other ear, then one tapped her nose. "Don't wander off."

The meadow behind the house was a trove of ancient relics. From the stone and clay artifacts she had found, to the century-old pear and apple trees next to the barn, to Quinn's house, the land showed signs of continuous habitation for hundreds of years. She had gotten into the habit of checking after the frequent small summer cloudbursts to see if anything new had turned up. The last time she had found a stone bowl and a long Indian smoking pipe, amazingly still intact.

Half an hour later she decided that the rain hadn't been hard enough when she noticed what looked like a pile of brown sticks. It wasn't until she got closer that she saw they were bones, darkened with age and the minerals in the black soil. The bones appeared to have been eroded out of the high bank of the creek that meandered through the meadow and probably would have washed away if they hadn't landed on a small sandbar. When the creek rose again after the next cloudburst, she was certain they would. At first she thought they were the bones of some medium-size animal, like a fox or a badger; then she saw the skull.

For a long time she just looked; then, hesitantly, she reached for the small human skull. It was intact, the teeth present. The lower jaw had become disconnected over time and lay on the sand. She counted the tiny teeth. There were twenty, with no gaps, indicating that the child had been old enough to have a full set of baby teeth, but not old enough to have begun losing them to make room for their adult replacements. After carefully setting the skull on the damp sand, she reached for one of the objects mixed with the bones. It was a small comb carved from a shell. Wetting her finger in the creek, she rubbed off a bit of the dirt clinging to the shell. It had been pink. There were other bits of shell, shaped like tiny birds with a hole drilled in each, shining whitely on the dark sand. Pieces of a tiny necklace, she thought, whatever had held them together long since rotted away. There was a small stone, streaked with pink and bright green, the kind a young child would think was precious. She picked up another object and rinsed it in the creek. Putting it to her lips, she blew the bone whistle, and several notes reminiscent of birdsong called over the meadow. She set it down and picked up a small stone bear—a favored toy, perhaps, or a guardian to protect the child on his final journey.

The last object was a ring. Brushing away the dirt clinging to it, she saw that it was made of gold and set with a tiny chip of turquoise. She knew the size of the finger that had worn it. For several moments she stared at the small brown bones; then slowly rose to her feet.

Engine sounds were still coming from the barn when Blue passed it. She went into the house and came back out with a striped blanket, pausing to pick up the shovel leaning against the wall before she started back to the meadow.

Nearly an hour later she finished arranging the small bones on the blanket, then placed the ring and other objects beside them. Carefully, she folded the edges of the blanket over and placed a handful of wild roses and sweet clover in the middle. Rising, she stood motionless for several minutes with her head bowed; then she reached for the shovel and began filling in the small grave, burying the child who had died hundreds of years in the past . . . and the one who had died three years ago.

Blue patted the last piece of meadow sod she had cut into place then sat back. After the next rain, there would be no sign of the grave. The tears began, slow and gentle for the first time. Those tiny trinkets bespoke a mother's love and loss. The mother had placed them with her child because they had been precious to him, as she would have done with her child had she had the chance.

She had kept her memories polished like precious jewels, afraid they would grow dull otherwise. That had been wrong, she knew now. They were supposed to grow dull. The unknown Indian mother had not mired herself in grief; circumstances would not have allowed her to. There had been food to gather and preserve, clothing to make, probably other children to care for—all the demands of life in that hard time to meet. Incapacitating grief would have been an unaffordable luxury.

There had been life here for centuries—first Indians, then pioneer women, followed by the women who had lived in the house that stood here now. They had lost children and husbands. They had grieved no less than she had, but they had picked up their lives again and gone on.

The grief of losing her husband and son would always be with her, and it was right that it should be, but as grief was a part of life and living, so were happiness and love... and the hope of perhaps another family someday. She had allowed grief to prevent her from finding them again, but this man and this place had shown her that she could open her heart again, love freely and wholeheartedly again. And that, even knowing the risks, it was worth it.

"Hey. Are you going to sleep out here all day?"

Awakened by the deep, gently chiding voice, Blue opened her eyes gradually. She felt as if she had been trapped in a dream of some cold dark place and finally woken to the sun and warmth again. She looked up at the man leaning over her, blocking out the sun overhead. The sun's warmth seemed to have sunk deep into her bones, and she felt the pulse of life in the meadow as her own. Slowly she raised her arms to him.

"Make love with me, Quinn."

His heart began to beat with a slow, heavy throbbing. Quinn could see the silvery traces of dried tears on her cheeks, but her blue eyes were clear and bright, the hollowness gone at last. She started to rise, and he put his hands on her shoulders to push her back down gently. "No, don't move," he said, his voice oddly tight.

She obeyed, relaxing back onto the soft mattress of grass. Catching her outstretched hands, he curled them into one of his and pressed them down over her head as his own head bent with agonizing slowness, giving her time to see how the sunlight glinted in his hair, how the planes of his face were taut and sharp, how his eyes glowed like molten silver.

The soft sighing of the breeze playing in the grass and the distant song of a meadowlark were the background music as time suspended its flow. The scents of warm earth and hot sun on fresh grass eddied around them. It was right that here in this beautiful meadow, a place that had seen so many generations of life, that she celebrate her return to it. She closed her eyes as his breath touched her lips, and the meadow slid into oblivion. His mouth devoured hers with slow greed, his tongue stroking over hers, then curling around it to draw it back into his mouth, his teeth raking over it.

His mouth left hers, and she felt him pulling away as he released her hands. With a sudden desperation, Blue curled up, reaching for him again.

"I'm not leaving, baby," he promised softly. Quinn found in himself a need that he'd never had before, a need to give pleasure and tenderness, to take with care and gentleness, that made his own gratification secondary. Easing her back down, he freed the first button of the boy's work shirt she wore, then the other four, finally spreading the shirt open. Releasing the front catch on her bra, he bared her breasts to the sun, pausing to savor the translucence of her fine-grained skin. He kissed her again, sliding his hands over the full mounds and stroking lightly until he heard her soft moan.

Blue lay quietly, absorbing new sensations. Each of his kindling touches ignited heat, until it felt as if the sun were inside her body. His mouth, surprisingly soft, grew gradually more insistent as it moved to her breast. He rolled the nipple between his tongue and teeth, nipping and soothing until passivity was impossible, and her back arched, her hands clenching in his hair as she tried to press his mouth even closer. All the while his hands worked lower, kneading and petting and shaping. Her jeans loosened, and she felt his roughened fingertips, then stiff denim and soft cotton sliding down her hips and thighs and calves, then only his hands sliding back up.

She had new scars on her knees—from saving his life. He touched his mouth to one, and she flinched as her hands gripped his shoulders, trying to pull him back up her body. Not because of any pain, Quinn knew, but because she wanted to hide them. With gentle persistence he kissed each one, the new and the old, and then the scars on her hands, silently telling her that he didn't see them as ugliness but as badges of courage and honor. When he looked up, her eyes were open and shimmering with tears. Leaning up, he kissed them closed, tasting the salt on his tongue.

Her hands skimmed across his belly; then he felt the delicate rasp of her nails over his chest as she dragged up his T-shirt. He helped her pull it over his head; then her hands were back at the snap of his jeans. Her fingers fumbled, and he took over the job, then moved between her legs. Her eyes were wide and brilliant as he probed her body gently. Coaxing her legs higher around him, he sank deeper, and her eyes drifted closed on a long sigh. Her arms closed around his shoulders, her fingers sliding into his hair, bringing his mouth down to hers. Her mouth was soft and giving, like her body as he took her in long, easy strokes. Setting his teeth against the moist, hot friction that threatened his control, he deliberately drew out the pleasure, building it, feeding on it until she was moaning mindlessly, on the threshold of ecstasy, but he wouldn't let either of them cross over quite yet. Watching her made him feel more a man than he ever had, yet it oddly humbled him, too. She didn't hold anything back but gave everything, and in giving, took more than he had ever given any other woman.

Long easy convulsions began rippling through her body, her smooth inner muscles and slick heat milking him, and suddenly he crossed over, too, not with a fiery ecstasy but with small soft endless explosions that shattered his soul.

Chapter 11

For three days they lived an idyllic illusion of normalcy—just two people with nothing more to do than catch up on a few chores, be lazy and make love. On the fourth morning, Blue knew the illusion was almost over. There was a subtly harder edge to him, although it was nothing she could specifically define. It was, she imagined, the change that came over a man as he prepared to go into battle.

She was reaching for his empty breakfast plate to clear it away when his hand on her arm stopped her. "Sit down," he said quietly.

"Tell me everything you remember from the time we walked into the casino for the meeting with Azziz until we left," he said when she was sitting across from him again. She saw the brief flare of heat in his eyes and knew he was thinking, too, of what had happened next.

This was the first time they had talked about what had happened in Atlantic City. For the first few weeks Quinn had known that she wasn't ready to, and for the past few days they had avoided it by tacit agreement, both of them knowing that once they did, their time here would be over.

An hour and a half later she had gone over it three times. It was the people he was interested in, of course, and, under his subtle interrogation, she found she remembered more than she thought. What, if anything, she remembered that he didn't, she had no way of knowing, as, for the first time in weeks, his eyes revealed nothing.

She rubbed absently at the dull ache overconcentration had created in the middle of her forehead. "One thing that still puzzles me is why the thief was so...theatrical. It was almost as if he actually were playing out a James Bond fantasy."

"I think he was."

She raised her head slowly to look at him. "You know who it is."

"I'm not absolutely certain. I need to check something out first."

She could see by his expression that he wasn't going to tell her who he suspected or what he still needed to find out. "And where will I be while you're checking it out?" Blue asked evenly.

"With me."

His answer surprised her, especially when she could see he didn't like it. She had been prepared to argue

with the one she had expected, but he had obviously
seen the same problem with leaving her behind that she
had: What if something happened and he didn't return? "When do we leave?"

This answer was even more clipped than the last.
"Tomorrow."

She merely nodded, then, standing up, changed the
subject. "Well, I better get breakfast cleaned up before it's time for lunch."

He stood up, too, as she began clearing the table.
For a moment he didn't move, and she sensed him
looking at her, as if there were something more he
wanted to say but when she glanced up, he was turning toward the door.

Blue set down the soldering iron and spool of lead
solder. While she gave the lead a few minutes to cool
completely, she put the tools and other items on the
rickety table into a shoe box. Two days before, they
had gone into town for the glass Quinn needed to repair the small window over the front door that had
broken during the winter. In the hardware store, on
the bargain table, she had seen a kit for making
stained-glass Christmas ornaments; it had seemed like
an omen. After persuading Quinn to buy a pane of
frosted glass as well as plain, she had set up shop in
one of the unused rooms, using the tools and copper
foil from the kit and two sawhorses and a piece of
leftover plywood.

Careful of the sharp edges, she held the square of
glass up to the light coming in the small dusty window. With only simple tools, she had had to use

simple design. From the frosted glass, she had cut five petal shapes, surrounding them with plain glass to complete the square. The incoming light shone through the square, giving the moonflower the same faint luminescence it had at night. She laughed softly. Although she hadn't consciously chosen the design for any reason other than that it was easy and a compliment to the real flowers, her subconscious, she suspected, had recognized the significance of choosing it for the first piece she had created in three years. Just like the moonflower vines, she was strong again.

"It's a beautiful piece of work."

Blue turned to see him standing in the doorway. "Thank you. It did turn out well, didn't it?" she said with a pleased smile.

Watching her lay the square of glass back down on the table, Quinn felt an intense satisfaction. She was creating again, not just repairing. "I'll go get the ladder and the putty," he said, "and then let's get some lunch in town."

After lunch at the little café, Blue understood the real reason behind his suggestion that they eat in town. Seemingly in no particular hurry to return to the farm, he strolled down the street. As they passed one of the little antique shops scattered along the main street, he paused to look in the window, then took her hand to lead her inside. He wanted, for one more afternoon, to preserve the illusion of normalcy. She was more than willing to pretend, too.

He was across the store looking through some old naval prints when she found the shelf of mechanical toys. "Quinn," she called softly, "come look."

Few of the toys were in good condition. Picking up a white cow spotted with rust, she tried to wind the key and discovered that the mechanism was either frozen or broken.

"That one's headed for the last wound-up," he murmured, taking the cow out of her hand and putting it back on the shelf.

For a minute she wasn't sure she'd heard what she'd thought she'd heard. "Quinn," she said with an astonished laugh, "you made a real joke!"

Raising one coal-black eyebrow, he looked at her. "I make jokes."

He sounded so honestly affronted that she laughed harder, which earned her another annoyed look.

Taking another toy, Quinn hid a smile. He had heard her laugh so seldom that he didn't care if it was at his expense.

Her laughter changed into a soft cry of appreciation when Blue saw what he held in his hands now. "Oh! Does it work?"

For an answer, Quinn wound both keys in the base of the toy, then flipped the level that controlled the movement of the figures. The music box unwound with a herky-jerky action that made the tune almost unidentifiable as "The Anniversary Waltz." After several false starts, the elderly couple froze in place while the clockwork screeched.

"Oh, what a shame." Taking the toy from him, Blue turned it over in her hands. It was sillier than most, since the elderly couple were mice dressed up in antiquated wedding finery, yet whoever had designed them had given them a solemn dignity and sweetly human expressions that made them oddly appealing. She looked up at him hopefully. "Do you think it could be fixed?"

"I doubt it. The music box sounds like a number of the teeth might be broken, and I suspect the clockwork is rusted pretty badly." Quinn saw her disappointment. "The outside's almost perfect, though. Do you want it?"

Setting the toy back on the shelf gently, she shook her head with a rueful laugh. "Thanks, but no. I think it would just frustrate me because I couldn't make it work." After a last look at the elderly mice, she turned her attention to a shelf of old paperweights.

They worked their way down the short main street and back up the other side. In the last shop, a couple and their two children followed them in. The little boy, who looked to be about nine, wore glasses that were slowly slipping down his nose until he pushed at the bridge with his finger to slide them back up.

The gesture triggered a memory, but it was a minute or two before she could crystallize it. It was someone she had thought she recognized, but he had been out of context, not where she was used to seeing him, and not looking like he normally did . . . and he had pushed at the bridge of his nose as if he were pushing a nonexistent pair of glasses back into place. Only his glasses were never sliding down; it was a nervous habit, Blue thought, as the face of the man at the chemin de fer table dissolved into the face of the man as she knew him. The face of a thief and a traitor.

Stunned at his identity, her eyes flew to Quinn for confirmation. He had been looking at the little boy, too.... His face grim, he nodded, and she knew he had seen what she had, and that the man was the one he suspected.

It was hard to believe that by this time tomorrow night it should all be over. Blue glanced across the Cherokee to the man behind the wheel. He had devised a trap, and they would set and spring it tomorrow. It was daring and unorthodox, but, as he had proved the night he had gotten them from Atlantic City to Washington, improvisation was another of his many talents. With the chance that they could be seized before they could spring the trap—and the possibility that others within Damage Control might be compromised—they couldn't risk approaching anyone for backup. They were on their own, but it wasn't an entirely unfamiliar situation, she thought sardonically, and they would each be doing what they were best at: Quinn setting and springing the trap, and she guarding his back.

He pulled the Cherokee up in back of the house, and Blue climbed out. Pausing, she looked out over the moon-silvered meadow. "It must be beautiful here in the winter, with the snow," she said softly.

Quinn came to stand behind her. "It is. I came up last January for a week. Even with the Jeep, I had to cover the last four miles on skis."

"That must have been fun. I've always wanted to learn how to cross-country ski."

Her smile, he saw, was unconsciously wistful. "I'll tea—" Ruthlessly he ground his teeth on the rest of the promise. Promises were for men who could keep them.

The smile gone as if it had never been, she turned silently and went into the house.

Blue went through the small refrigerator, cleaning out the perishables. Fortunately there wasn't much that would have to be wasted. Because they were going to leave early in the morning, the house had to be readied tonight to be closed up for another indefinite period. Quinn was out in the barn now, securing the Model T. They had taken it out for a test run on a back road, where it had proved itself to truly be a windup car by dying with clockwork regularity.

She turned off the gas to the old stove, then, finished in the kitchen, started through the house, checking windows to see that they were locked on the inside after Quinn had closed the shutters outside to secure the house for another long absence. After latching the window in the room that she had used as a temporary workshop, she picked up the shoe box that held her tools and supplies. Then she set it down again. It had seemed like an omen when she found it in the hardware store; maybe leaving it here would be another kind of omen—that she would return.

She had heard the words he'd bitten off. *I'll teach you next winter.* Would they have a next winter? Would they have a day-after-tomorrow? She had no illusions that Quinn's plan was without risks; it was dangerous. She had no illusions about the showdown to come afterward, either, and that one was going to be even riskier, because there was absolutely no guarantee of success. She wanted another marriage, more children, and the man she wanted them with was Quinn Eisley.

She firmly believed that she would have fully returned to life on her own, but there was no denying that he had sped up the process. He had been the catalyst, but, unlike a true catalyst, he had been changed, too. He had purposely isolated himself, walled himself off to human emotion and human need, but she had found a few cracks, tiny ones to be sure, but cracks just the same, and she intended to pry them open wider until he let her in. And when she got in, she wasn't fool enough to think the battle would be over. She knew she would have to cope with the demands and dangers of the work he had committed his life to and the restrictions that work would place on her own life, but there were accommodations they both could make that wouldn't lessen his effectiveness. She would have to teach him to love openly, to fully trust her, to *talk* to her, and she knew now she would never be completely successful—but complete success wasn't necessary to build the good life that she was convinced they could have together. The next battle would be to convince him.

Passing the front door, she glanced up at the luminous moonflower. She was strong again; she just hoped she was strong enough.

Quinn walked through the darkened, silent house. When he had come out of the shower, he had found the small lamp on in the bedroom and the bed turned down, but no Blue. Seeing the back door open, he moved silently through the kitchen to the open door way. She was standing motionless on the porch, wearing the white T-shirt she'd appropriated for a nightgown, her beautiful long legs exposed. The shirt was a waste of time; she might as well have left it off for all the time she was going to wear it, yet he derived a certain pleasure in seeing her in his clothes. She was looking toward the meadow, in her hand, one of the white flowers from the vines she had rescued. The sweet sultry scent of the flowers was so close to hers that they might be the same. It enveloped him as hers always did, and the low perpetual throbbing in his groin increased.

"Blue."

At the sound of his rough voice, she turned around. Her face pale, with the ethereal luminosity of the flowers, and her eyes dark and fathomless, she came toward him soundlessly. In the white shirt, she looked almost like an otherworldly spirit, but it was a very real woman who walked into his arms.

Blue swayed against him, and his hands caught her, stroking around to the small of her back, rubbing slow circles as his mouth took hers with a leisurely, plundering deliberation. The darkness had hidden the fact that he was naked, but she realized it when she felt him hard and insistent against her belly. Wrapping her arms around his neck, she pressed closer, her tongue dueling with his stroke for stroke. His arms shifted, one sliding down beneath her hips, the other up to her shoulders, and he lifted her, never breaking the seal of their mouths.

Stretching her out on the bed, he stripped off the T-shirt before lying down beside her. She saw his eyes

soften from silver to smoke as she reached for him.
Leaning over her, he began kissing her again, her
mouth, the hollow beneath her ear, the side of her
throat, the curve of her shoulder, while his hand made
a slow sweep of her body from shoulder to knee. Blue
found the scars on his body that were the campaign
ribbons other men wore on their chests—the puckered white circle high on his shoulder, the livid weals
on his ribs and his thigh, the jagged furrow down his
back and the still-reddened fist-size star on his chest.
She gave silent thanks again that he had survived each
battle and swallowed the tears burning the back of her
throat.

His mouth reached her breast, and he suckled with
a strong, unhurried rhythm, his tongue finessing the
nipple to an exquisitely aching hardness. Her fingers
tangled in his hair to hold that deliciously torturing
mouth in place. It moved, and she started to moan
with disappointment; then his lips closed around her
other breast, setting up the same devastatingly relaxed rhythm again that was drawing every nerve in
her body taut. She was so lost in the slow, seductive
pull and release that she was only dimly aware of his
hand slipping inside her panties, searching down.
Suddenly, every grain of attention and every nerve in
her body was focused between her thighs as his hand
unerringly found what it had been seeking.

"Quinn—" Her voice was caught between whimper and demand as his thumb began to rub and circle
and press. His teeth nipped at a nipple that was already ultrasensitive, and the combined sensations were
almost more than she could bear. Suddenly one long

finger penetrated, deepening and escalating the rhythm of his mouth on her breast. Her body jolted, and her hands clutched frantically at his shoulders as she teetered on the edge of ecstasy.

"Easy, easy," he breathed in a low rasp. "Not yet. Not until I'm inside you." Quinn ground his teeth together as she surged against his hand, almost fracturing his control. She was going to be as hungry for him as he was for her. Over the past few days, he'd discovered that, no matter how many times he had her, the hunger didn't abate; it only intensified, and he wanted her to know that same insatiable hungering.

A second finger joined the first, and Blue strained toward him helplessly with a moaning cry. Suddenly his pleasuring hand was gone, and she felt as well as heard the tearing of cloth as her panties were ripped away. The silky hair on his thighs brushed against the smoothness of hers as he kneed her legs open and fitted himself between them. She raced avid hands over strong thighs roped with long muscles, lean hips and a hard broad chest. Then she shivered, her fingers curling into the soft mat of hair when he ran his palm over her stomach and down, his low rough whisper making dark, carnal promises. Catching her gaze, he held it as he thrust into her, one deliciously, torturously, slow inch at a time, and her breath fled from her lungs. He filled her hard and deep, then withdrew as slowly as he had entered. He kept to the same frustrating beat, and her hands slid down to his flexing buttocks to urge him to a quicker pace.

His eyes intent on her face, gauging every nuance of expression as her eyes closed and her head rolled back

and forth slowly on the pillow, Quinn subtly increased the speed of advance and withdrawal. Her hips
met his at every stroke, drawing him deeper and
deeper. She was an all-eager, giving woman—eager
only for him, giving only to him. Her hips surged
against his without warning, smashing his careful
control, and he began driving into her, the soft wet
pulse of her body closing around him, absorbing him,
and he cried out hoarsely as he sank into her one last
time, lost in the intolerable pleasure of her.

Blue lay still, relishing every inch of him against her
and within her. As both their hearts slowed to a less
frenetic beat, she felt the subtle resonance vibrating
between them that was more than physical surfeit. The
three words that she said with her body each time he
reached for her, cried silently in her heart and trem-
bled on her tongue, unspoken.

Quinn gazed down at the woman sleeping in a patch
of moonlight. If he had ever had any true happiness
in his life, it had come during these past few weeks
with Blue. He closed his eyes against the sudden aching tightness in his chest. Dear God, he didn't think he
could bear to have it end, but he had no choice. They
should have left three days ago, when he knew she had
recovered from the trauma of the warehouse fire, but
he hadn't been able to bring himself to give up the all-
consuming joy and peace he had found in her arms,
feeling that eclipsed even a physical satisfaction that
was unlike any he had ever known before. He felt a
oneness with her that he had never felt with any other

human being, had never expected to feel and knew he would never feel again.

In the most traditional way, he wanted her for his own—the conventional forsaking of all others, until death did them part. And it was the one thing he couldn't have. He had only to ask, he knew, and she would give him what he wanted. He felt it in the total giving of her body, saw it in the honest emotion in her eyes. There was an exquisitely brutal torture in knowing it and knowing he couldn't ask. He laid his hand gently on her bare stomach, savoring the contrast of his darker hand against her pale skin. He wanted to plant his seed inside her, watch her belly grow big, know that there was a part of him, of them, growing in her. He wanted to catch the baby as it slid out of her, hold it in his hands and know that both the baby and the mother were his. And he never would.

He could see himself in the years ahead with Christian and Erin Dekker's little girl, the bachelor uncle like Nelson had been to Blue, accepted but never quite part of the inner intimate circle of love and family, and he felt a hopeless, furious despair. That wasn't what he wanted—but it was all he would ever have, because dreams belonged to other men, men who were listed in the phone book, men who had subscriptions to the local paper because they were home every night to read it—men who didn't have other men hunting them. Those men could afford the luxury of dreams.

Gently he brushed a dark curl off her faintly flushed cheek. Already she had proved how dangerous she was. Never had he allowed anything to distract him from his job, never had he put someone's safety—including his own—ahead of the mission, and he had already done it, twice, because of her. And he would do it again. Once he had tried and failed to imagine the depth of feeling that had driven her husband to the desperate act of throwing her through a second-story window to save her life. Now he could imagine it easily. He would trade his soul to keep her safe.

He hadn't been having sex, as he'd tried to convince himself; he'd been making love, for the first time in his life. He loved her, and now he knew what hell was. It was having everything you'd ever wanted in your grasp and knowing you had to let it go. As he went down into the final darkness, his last word would be her name, his last vision would be her—the image of the one chance of happiness he'd had and had to destroy—before it destroyed him.

Her eyes opened suddenly, and she smiled up at him. Her hand reached for his and drew it down to her mouth, pressing a soft warm kiss in his palm. He rolled onto her, and her hips shifted to cradle him. Easing into her, he began to move. Looking down, he memorized the expression of exalted pleasure on her face. It was the last time he would see it, would feel her arms tighten around him, her hands slide over his back. It was the last time he would fill his hands with her breasts, the last time her body would clasp his, the last time he would feel her shudder and tremble with fulfillment. The last time he would die and be reborn in her arms.

Chapter 12

"There goes one of the clerks," Quinn muttered.

"And there are no customers in the store right now," Blue murmured.

"Okay, let's go."

Quinn had the door of the Cherokee open when her hand stopped him. Turning his head, he gave her an inquiring look. "Remember, Quinn," she instructed. "Stay out of the way and keep your mouth shut."

For a split second, his expression was blank; then she saw a rare grin. Cupping her chin in his hand, he gave her a swift, hard kiss. "I'll remember."

She crossed the suburban Baltimore street alone, knowing Quinn would follow in a few minutes. When he had first suggested this plan, she had thought he was joking, but after thinking it over, she had realized that, while it was almost too simple, it had an excellent chance of success, and it solved several problems. She passed several storefronts, then pulled open the door of an electronics-and-computer store.

The salesman met her in the middle of the store. "Can I help you, ma'am?"

She frowned at him vaguely. "Well, I've been thinking about getting a computer, and one of my friends has one of yours and really likes it, but I don't really know very much about them...." She let her voice trail off to give the impression that she still had her doubts about the whole idea but could be convinced, and his salesman's instincts went into high gear, as she had hoped.

"It is confusing, what with laptops and hard disks and floppies and modems and everything, I know," he sympathized, "but you came to the right place, ma'am." He began walking toward the back of the store to the computers on display, and she followed dutifully. "Why don't you let me show you what I have? I don't want you to buy anything today," he admonished, and she managed to keep a straight face. "Just take a look, and then you can go home and think it over." He stopped beside a computer setup that would have them facing the front of the store. "Now, this is a nice little start—"

"I'd like to see that one," Blue interrupted him, pointing to a computer display that faced the back of the store. "That's the kind my friend has," she explained.

"Sure," the salesman agreed heartily, and she could see him mentally figuring his commission already. "This is a real nice machine." He held the chair in front of the computer for her and pulled up another for himself. "Does just about everything but the dishes."

He laughed at his own joke, and, wincing, Blue forced herself to laugh, too. To further her image of a computer illiterate, she had chosen a plain skirt and blouse at the discount store they had stopped at earlier, and apparently it was working. She folded her hands primly in front of her, glancing in the tiny mirror she had concealed in her palm in time to see Quinn opening the door. "Well, what does all of this do?" she said a little loudly to cover the sound of the door.

"Well, this switch turns on the drive, and this one the monitor."

She gave him a helpless look, and he launched into a lengthy explanation of drive options and the advantages of a color monitor over a monochrome one. Adjusting her hands casually, she followed Quinn's progress in the mirror as he disappeared into the office behind the sales counter. He had decided that the noon hour would be the best time to visit the store, since clerks would be out to lunch and customers would be scarce. After scouting several, they had settled on this one, since it was staffed with only two salesmen and there had been only a handful of customers all morning.

"Well, what do you think?"

Blue smiled at him brightly. "I think I'd like to see it in action."

Obligingly, the salesman began running a spreadsheet program, keeping up his patter as the numbers shifted. Quinn was setting up his trap the same way the traitor had set up his thefts—by computer. To do it, all he needed was to send a message, and he had two choices of how to do it: buying the necessary computer and modem—renting was out, since neither of them had any identification—then setting up in a motel, at the risk of being traced and found before they could spring the trap, or "borrowing" it. Because of the necessity of networking with other stores, any chain computer store, he had figured, should have what he needed in the office.

Quinn tapped in the codes and waited, hoping that they hadn't been changed. He was sure those that were needed to get into the computer bank had been, but those on people's personal terminals might have stayed the same. Or they might have been left in effect just to see who was calling, he thought sardonically. Access was cleared, and he typed a short message to P. K. Walther: *I have something that belongs to you.* He added the time and place, then cleared the screen.

Leaving the computer terminal, he gave the store a quick scan and saw that Blue still had the salesman's undivided attention. Quickly he picked up the phone and began dialing. This message, one that he hadn't mentioned to her, couldn't go by computer, because Nelson refused to use one. It was a risk, but he calculated that the odds were in his favor—just. After th

first eleven digits, the number for a long-distance call,
the phone rang once. A pleasant female voice told him
that it was 12:42 p.m. and eighty-nine degrees Fahr-
enheit in Washington, D.C. He dialed two more numbers and there was a click and a dial tone, as if he had
been disconnected. He waited, and after thirty seconds there was another click, and the phone began
ringing. It was answered on the third ring, and he delivered the same message, then hung up. The call
would be traced, of course, but he doubted Nelson
would waste manpower sending anyone here when he
knew where he could find them a few hours from now.

The salesman had a game on the screen when Blue
saw Quinn leave the office. He was halfway to the
door when she saw a couple through the glass, about
to come in. "Here, let me try," she said quickly,
grabbing the mouse and pressing just a fraction too
late. The screen exploded in fireworks, and a razzing
chorus of beeps and whistles announced her inept-
ness. "I'm sorry," she said contritely.

The salesman summoned up a smile. "That's okay.
Now—"

The beeps and whistles had covered the sound of the
door opening, but the salesman caught movement out
of the corner of his eye and turned to see the couple
browsing through answering machines and the door
closing behind Quinn. "Say, I didn't see that big,
dark-haired guy come in, did you?" he asked her.

She looked around vaguely. "Where?" Before he
could answer, she stood up. "You've been very help-
ful—" she glanced at the nameplate on his white shirt

"—Mark, but I feel guilty taking up any more of your time, especially when you have other customers. I'm going to take your advice and go home and think about it."

Minutes later, after a block of window shopping just in case the salesman happened to glance out the window, she opened the passenger door of the Cherokee. As soon as she pulled it closed, Quinn started the engine. "Did you get it sent?" she asked as he pulled away from the curb.

He nodded briefly. "Now we'll find out if it was received."

Blue looked across the grassy Mall. The Smithsonian museums bordering it had been closed for half an hour, thinning the summer crowds, but a number of people were still using the Mall as the large park that it essentially was. There were the usual joggers, roller bladers and Frisbee players, a few families and people sitting alone or together on the benches. A desultory whiffle ball game was in progress, and the lone hot-dog vendor was doing a brisk business. Stopping for a set of hamstring stretches, she checked to make sure the tall, dark-haired man in the jeans and black shirt sitting on the bench directly in front of the red Smithsonian Castle was still reading his newspaper. Quinn had felt the Castle would appeal to "P. K. Walther's" fondness for theatrics as a meeting place, and the open, populated space lessened any chance of an ambush, even if he'd had time to find the men to set one up.

Putting her foot on a nearby bench, she retied her running shoe. She had exchanged her skirt and blouse for shorts and a tank top to make her one of the anonymous joggers, although she had one accessory she imagined few, if any, of them had—in the belt pack around her waist was a small pistol that Quinn had produced from under the Cherokee's front seat. He was armed with the gun he'd brought out of the warehouse. As he had checked the clip a final time, she had seen the same look on his face that she'd seen the night he was stalking the men in the warehouse—cold and hard and predatory, his eyes flat and empty.

She was straightening up when she felt a hard, round object in the small of her back. For a heartbeat or two she froze; then, very slowly, she turned around. "Hello, Hal."

Quinn frowned as he glanced over his newspaper toward the bench where Blue had been tying her shoe. She couldn't have disappeared that fast. Damning the dusky light that made it hard to pick out details, he searched the Mall, then saw her heading diagonally toward him, walking close beside the Librarian. Cursing steadily under his breath, he forced himself to wait until the information kiosk a dozen feet away hid them from each others' view for a few scant seconds.

"Where is he? I saw him here right up until a minute ago."

Hal Ladwig punctuated each sentence with a sharp jab of the gun he held in her ribs.

"I don't know, Hal. I don't see him now, either," she said with careful reasonableness. Remembering the man in evening clothes, his hair slicked back in a ponytail that she had seen in the casino, Blue felt the same sense of unreality now as she looked at him with horn-rims, straight straggling hair, rumpled khakis and a plaid shirt. The gun, though, was very real.

"He has to be here." He let go of her arm to push at his glasses, then seemed to forget to take hold of it again. "He can't just have disappeared." He jerked his head to look over his shoulder to make sure no one was sneaking up behind him. Her fingers were easing open the zipper on her belt pack when a familiar hand grabbed her arm, and suddenly she was flying through the air.

She landed about six feet away and would have fallen if not for the hot-dog vendor, who seemed to have abruptly abandoned his cart. Looking up, she recognized him as one of the backup team from Atlantic City; then, glancing around, she saw that the two Frisbee players, the maintenance man who had been working on the carousel and the jogger converging on Quinn and Hal Ladwig were familiar, too. Even more so was the stocky, middle-aged man she'd earlier given only passing notice as he sat on a nearby bench, his head slumped on his chest, his straw fedora hiding his face, seemingly napping.

"John," she said in startled surprise as he took over from the hot-dog vendor, wrapping a steadying arm around her shoulder.

"Are you all right?" he asked gruffly.

She nodded. He studied her for a minute, as if to verify it for himself, then removed his arm from her shoulder and took her elbow to guide her toward the small circle of men.

Hal Ladwig and Quinn stood in the middle. No guns were in sight, and, glancing around, Blue realized that no one appeared to have noticed anything unusual. As she joined the circle, her eyes met Quinn's, and the killing rage she saw stunned her. As he looked her over, seemingly reassuring himself that she was all right just as John had, it faded only a little.

Hal Ladwig suddenly started talking, seemingly to no one in particular. "I was afraid of this. I'm better at planning than execution, but I didn't have time to find anyone else to handle it." He paused to push tiredly at his glasses. "When I got the message over my computer this afternoon, I couldn't think who had sent it. Then I thought of you." When the Librarian's myopic eyes focused on him, Quinn saw the insanity in them, and the raging violence he'd felt at the sight of the gun aimed at Blue began to drain away. "I always suspected you didn't die in that fire. You're just too hard to kill, Eisley," he added with a faint note of complaint. "I was hoping," he rambled on, "when you said you had something that belonged to me, that you had the guns, but—" he shrugged with a rueful grimace "—I guess not."

The eyes around the circle reflected the horror he felt, Quinn knew, not at encountering the evil they had expected, but something worse—the disintegration of a once rational mind.

"Why, Hal?" Nelson asked in a tone that was oddly gentle.

"For years I've watched everyone else go out on missions while I never left headquarters. I knew I'd never get a chance to work in the field, so I made my own," he said simply. He was silent for a few moments; then he frowned down at the hand he was cradling as if he had just noticed it. "You know, Quinn, I think you broke my wrist," he said conversationally.

He didn't say anything else, and after a minute, in response to Nelson's silent signal, the Frisbee players led him away.

Blue closed her eyes, fighting the exhaustion that had come with the hours of debriefing. The door to the conference room swung inward, and she opened her eyes slowly to see Quinn coming in.

"How bad is it?" she asked. She knew they had been running checks on the computer systems to determine what, if any, damage Hal Ladwig had done.

"Bad enough," he said grimly. "Damage Control is going to have to do some damage control on itself."

Turning, he pushed in the button on the doorknob and closed the door, locking it. Blue sat up straighter, feeling the tension starting to tighten her body. This wasn't the time or place she would have chosen to make her stand, but it appeared the choice had been taken out of her hands.

His expression was blank, as usual, but she had learned to read him, and now she saw the wariness and caution in his eyes, as if he felt he had to protect himself from her. "As of five minutes ago, you retired," he said abruptly.

She nodded. "I never intended this to be a permanent career." If the showdown had to be now, she wasn't going to postpone it any longer, Blue decided. "I intend for you to be my permanent career," she said with a slight smile.

Don't let her say the words, Quinn pleaded silently. "You've had a rough time," he said expressionlessly. "It's understandable that you might mistake gratitude for something else. It's also easy to get caught up in the excitement of the moment. Once it wears off, you realize that's all it was—and sex."

If it was just a case of being noble, he could be cured of it, but she was afraid it was more than that. Ever since they had left the farm, she had sensed a sadness, almost a despair in him. She stood up to put them on more equal footing. "Yes, I'm grateful to you, Quinn," she began quietly. "You helped me through a difficult time, but I know the difference between gratitude and love." She saw the flicker in his eyes, almost of acute pain. "I also know the difference between the 'excitement of the moment,' fantastic sex," she added with a ghost of a smile, "and love." She saw the flicker again, stronger this time. "I was married, if you recall."

He seized on it, despite what the words cost him. "Don't confuse me with your husband," he said with a sneer.

"I don't," Blue said evenly. "I will never love you as I loved him."

Pain could be controlled, Quinn reminded himself; he just had to disconnect it.

"Just as I never loved him as I love you. I love you, Quinn," she repeated, then paused a beat. "And you love me. You're just afraid to admit it."

For a moment she thought her taunt would have no effect; then emotion slowly became visible in his eyes, and she almost cried out at the mixture of pain and desperation she saw.

His hands jerked out and tightened brutally on her shoulders, and she almost cried out again. "Yes, I love you, and yes, I'm afraid!" he admitted furiously. "I haven't trusted anyone but myself in years, and now I'm the last person I can trust. To keep you safe, I would give up every secret I know, every man in Damage Control, the whole damned country." He paused, fighting for control. Easing his hurtful grip on her shoulders, he went on more quietly. "I've never loved another woman, and I never will again, but there can be nothing, absolutely no connection, between us, because you could be used to get to me. I have to know you're safe, Blue." His hands tightened again as he shook her slightly. "It's the only way I can live, the only way I can work."

She heard the agony behind his words, saw the bleak hopelessness in his eyes, and her heart ached fo

him, for both of them, for what he was so determined
to deny them. He lived by an iron code that had no
room for compromise. Compromise was possible, she
knew, but she also knew he wouldn't listen to rational
arguments now, wouldn't discuss changes he could
make in his work, adjustments they could make in
their life-style, so that they could both be safe—
changes and adjustments that would be minor compared to the rich life they could have together. He had
to reach the compromise on his own. She had to gam-
ble that time, time spent without her, would be her
best argument.

Twisting free, Blue stepped away from him and
moved to the door. "Very well, Quinn." She was
proud of the steadiness of her voice. "I can live without you." She paused to make sure she had his attention. "I just don't want to."

As she walked down the hall away from him, she
had told herself she would give him six months; if he
didn't come to her then, she would go to him and give
it one more try. On the long Metro ride home, six
months had become five. As she had stepped off the
second of the Woodley Park Station escalators, five
became four. Closing the door of her apartment,
which had seemed to only open her further to the pain
she was trying to ignore, she had decided three months
would be enough.

Now those three months had almost passed, Blue
thought, with no call, no visit, no word from him of
any kind, and the loneliness and loss didn't decrease

as the days dwindled down, she found. She had told him she could live without him, and she hadn't lied. She could; she just had to accept that the renewed promise of her life would never be fully realized without him.

For a while she had cherished the hope that one promise might be. The first time they had made love, and again in the meadow, they had used no protection, but that hope had been dashed one morning a few weeks ago, and she had known another aching sense of loss.

At first she thought he might have returned to one of the world's killing fields out of some perverted sense of atonement, deliberately putting himself in harm's way, but almost as instantly as she had thought it, she had known that was one fear she needn't have. Quinn Eisley had no latent death wishes; life, no death, was the strongest force in him.

Still, she did wonder if he'd left Washington, until John had destroyed that fantasy and she'd had to face the possibility that she had gambled and lost. Perhaps his need, his love, simply wasn't as strong as she had thought—or his self-denial was stronger. She could face it, but she had to know it with absolute certainty, she thought as she turned up the narrow Georgetown street.

Perhaps he would sell the place, Quinn thought. The vines growing up the back porch were brown now, the last flowers nipped by an early frost, yet their scent still seemed to pervade the house. Only it wasn't the scent of the flowers, he knew. It was her scent, just like it was the sound of her laughter, her phantom warmth and softness in his bed, that haunted the house, haunted him. And if he sold this house, he would have to sell the one in Georgetown, too, because, despite the few hours she'd spent there, she was there, too.

What had she said? That she could live without him—she just didn't want to? Then she was stronger than he was. He had tried to disconnect the pain, but all the tricks he'd learned for shutting out physical pain didn't work with this kind, he'd discovered. The want and need were a gnawing ache that was slowly eating him alive, slowly killing him.

Five hours later, he cut the engine of the Jeep. Picking up the object sitting on the seat beside him, he stared at it for a long minute. He was coming on a fool's errand, he knew, as the old fears and doubts began to assail him once more, making the decision that had seemed so right a few hours ago suddenly seem wrong. Not giving himself any more time to think, he shoved open the Jeep door.

Blue debated answering the knock on the door. She was in the middle of a complicated piece that she was designing as she went along, and interruptions destroyed her concentration. At least, that was the excuse she gave herself. The knock came again, the hand on the other side of the door more impatient, and she finally started for the door. It might be John, she thought with a trace of guilt. He had taken to coming by more often and dropping the name Quinn Eisley into the conversation with odd frequency, considering that she had once sensed his disapproval of anything but a professional relationship between Quinn and herself.

Opening the door, she almost thought she must have conjured him up out of her earlier disappointment at not finding him home. "Hello, Quinn," she said guardedly.

"Blue." She held the door open in silent invitation, and he walked into the apartment. Shutting the door behind him, she studied him covertly. He looked as if he had lost weight; his face was thinner. He didn't look as if he had come to say anything she wanted to hear.

Coming to stand in front of him, she saw what he had in his hand. "Oh! Did you decide it could be fixed after all?"

Quinn held the mechanical toy out to her. "It just took a little more work than usual," he said neutrally. Seeing her again had been a mistake. One glance and he was almost sick with hunger for her.

Blue wound the two keys, then set the toy on the table. "The Anniversary Waltz" played smoothly, with only a few missed notes as the elderly mouse couple whirled with slow stateliness and never a misstep. "You did a wonderful job," she said softly.

His hand dismissed the compliment, then waved negligently again when she tried to hand the toy back to him after it wound down. "Keep it. I got it for you."

"Thank you," she said, setting it back down carefully, then turned to face him. "Did you just come to give me the toy, Quinn?" If it hadn't been for the toy, she didn't think she would have had the courage to ask.

She saw the bleakness come back into his eyes just before he spoke. "Nothing's changed, Blue."

She nodded slowly. "I see." Suddenly she was furious, furious with him for being so rigidly uncompromising, and furious with herself for even thinking of accepting it. She had backed off last time, but not this time, by God. This time she was going to fight as dirty as she could, because if she lost him this time, she knew she had lost him forever. "So. You're still determined to give me up. Well, I appreciate you coming to tell me that, Quinn. Now that I know for certain, I'm free to find another man."

His hand lashed out with shocking speed and closed with gentle but inexorable possession around her throat. "Damn you, Blue." His voice was a low snarl. "You do, and I'll—"

"You'll what? You're giving me up, remember?" she reminded him. "I'm free—"

"I'll kill any man who touches you." His voice was flat and utterly convincing. "You're—"

She stood quietly, his hand still locked around her throat as he struggled with himself, a vein throbbing jerkily in his neck, his mouth pulling into a tight slash. He could snap her neck with a mere twist of his wrist, but she felt no fear, because she knew he would never harm her. "What am I, Quinn?" she prodded him softly.

A spasm of emotion racked his entire body; then he suddenly relaxed, the struggle resolved, and she waited, half dreading his answer. "Mine." His sigh sounded oddly like one of profound relief. "You're mine, Blue, and I can't let you go. I love you," he said, speaking the words of unconditional surrender, and, in doing so, claimed total victory.

Epilogue

'Hi, sailor."

He slipped his hands under the T-shirt she had put n after her shower. After three years she still stole his othes. He ran his hands over her smooth abdomen d up to capture her breasts, savoring the warm eight on his palms as she leaned back against him, e hair dryer in her hand forgotten. He met her eyes the bathroom mirror and frowned as he nuzzled her r. "What's your name again?" he asked.

Her giggle turned into a soft moan as his thumbs bbed slow circles. "What time are we meeting the kkers?" he murmured, watching her eyes grow avy in the mirror.

"Seven-thirty," she murmured back; then her eyes

opened wide, and she jerked away from him. "An
it's six-thirty now!"

He hauled her back for a brief hard kiss. "Remem
ber where we left off," he murmured against he
mouth, then set her away from him and leaned dow
to switch the hair dryer back on. "I'll take care o
Michael," he said, raising his voice, and saw her no
and smile.

Twenty minutes later Blue followed the sound c
high-pitched squeals and deep laughter coming fro
the nursery. Minutes earlier it had been coming fro
the bathroom as her husband gave their son a batl
Peeking around the corner, she saw Quinn, wearin
just a towel, sitting in the bentwood rocker gentl
tossing his eleven-month-old son, who was wearin
nothing, into the air. It was a favorite after-bath gam
between the two of them, although she always pr
dicted diaperless disaster, but Michael's manners we
much better with his father, she thought wryly.

As she watched them, she felt the familiar tightne
in her chest. Three years ago today, on her weddi
day, she hadn't dared dream that life could be so goo
The last three years hadn't been all roses, to be su
Quinn Eisley hadn't magically become an open, co
municative, tractable man overnight. There were
strictions on their lives that other families didn't ha
although his promotion shortly before they were m
ried had taken him out of the field and direct dang
The prices she had paid, however, were small wl
measured against the rewards.

Quinn glanced up suddenly and grinned at her as if he had known she was there all the time. He probably had, she thought as she grinned back for no more reason than sheer happiness.

Silently Quinn watched his wife undress. *His wife*. The words had never meant more than they did tonight. The past three years had not been easy for her, he knew. She had said she would never ask him for explanations he couldn't give concerning his work, and she hadn't, but because she didn't ask, he knew he sometimes asked for more than was fair for her to give. It was a prime reason that he had found it much easier to give up fieldwork than he had expected.

Tonight they had celebrated their anniversary with good friends, but it was the private celebration that he had been looking forward to all day. She hadn't wanted a present, she had told him, because she already had everything she could possibly want. He had gotten her a diamond anyway, for her right hand, but tonight, after he had taken the edge off a hunger that dinner had done nothing to satisfy, when she was soft and warm and sated in his arms, he was going to give her her real present. He was going to give her a past to connect with the future they were building together—her father. Nelson had finally agreed. It was a small enough gift for all she had given him that he had never thought he would have—a son, true happiness, peace, and a love that burned with a steady, eternal flame.

Blue opened her eyes to see pure love burning bright and strong in eyes that had once been cold and empty. The molten pleasure built, each stroke hotter and higher, until it consumed her body and soul, and joyfully she followed him into the fire.

*   *   *   *   *

AMERICAN HERO

You have spoken! You've asked for more of our irresistible American Heroes, and now we're happy to oblige. After all, we're as in love with these men as you are! In coming months, look for these must-have guys:

In COLD, COLD HEART (IM #487) by Ann Williams, we're looking at a hero with a heart of ice. But when faced with a desperate mother and a missing child, his heart begins to melt. You'll want to be there in April to see the results!

In May we celebrate the line's tenth anniversary with one of our most-requested heroes ever: Quinn Eisley. In QUINN EISLEY'S WAR (IM #493) by Patricia Gardner Evans, this lone-wolf agent finally meets the one woman who is his perfect match.

The weather starts to heat up in June, so come deep-sea diving with us in Heather Graham Pozzessere's BETWEEN ROC AND A HARD PLACE (IM #499). Your blood will boil right along with Roc Trellyn's when he pulls in his net to find—his not-quite-ex-wife!

AMERICAN HEROES. YOU WON'T WANT TO MISS A SINGLE ONE—ONLY FROM

INTIMATE MOMENTS®
Silhouette®

IMHER04

Take 4 bestselling love stories FREE

Plus get a FREE surprise gift!

Special Limited-time Offer

Mail to Harlequin Reader Service®

3010 Walden Avenue
P.O. Box 1867
Buffalo, N.Y. 14269-1867

YES! Please send me 4 free Silhouette Intimate Moments® novels and my free surprise gift. Then send me 6 brand-new novels every month, which I will receive months before they appear in bookstores. Bill me at the low price of $2.71* each plus 25¢ delivery and applicable sales tax, if any.* I understand that accepting the books and gift places me under no obligation ever to buy any books. I can always return a shipment and cancel at any time. Even if I never buy another book from Silhouette, the 4 free books and the surprise gift are mine to keep forever.

245 BPA AJCK

Name	(PLEASE PRINT)	
Address	Apt. No.	
City	State	Zip

**Silhouette Books
is proud to present
our best authors,
their best books…
and the best in
your reading pleasure!**

Throughout 1993, look for exciting books
by these top names in contemporary
romance:

CATHERINE COULTER—
Aftershocks in February

FERN MICHAELS—
Nightstar in March

DIANA PALMER—
Heather's Song in March

ELIZABETH LOWELL
Love Song for a Raven in April

SANDRA BROWN
(previously published under
the pseudonym Erin St. Claire)—
Led Astray in April

LINDA HOWARD—
All That Glitters in May

When it comes to passion,
we wrote the book.

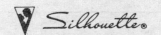

BOBT1RR

INTIMATE MOMENTS®

10TH

Anniversary

Celebrate our anniversary with a fabulous collection of firsts....

Silhouette Books is proud to present a FREE hardbound collection of the first Silhouette Intimate Moments® titles written by three of your favorite authors:

NIGHT MOVES   by *New York Times* best-
                        selling author
                        Heather Graham
                        Pozzessere
LADY OF THE NIGHT   by Emilie Richards
A STRANGER'S SMILE   by Kathleen Korbel

This unique collection will not be available in retail stores and is only available through this exclusive offe

INTIMATE MOMENTS®

10TH

Anniversary

ONE PROOF OF PURCHASE

082 K